THE
TRUNK KEY

CAROLYN NASH

Carolyn Nash

Jannie L Crist

DEDICATION

Always and forever
To my boys.

And to
Amy Redd-Greiner
Katie Fox
Leland Dirks

Great friends
Great critics
Great writers

CHAPTER 1

"Look, Amy, I'm going to Donut World. Do you want something or not? I can't keep talking on this thing while I'm driving."

"But you've been so good! And why aren't you using your ear bud?"

"I am using my ear bud," I said. "I just don't like talking and driving at the same time. Makes me nervous. And are you kidding? I've been the Mother Teresa of dieting. But now I'm going to be Scarlett O'Hara." I raised one fist toward the ceiling of the van and shook it. "I want a chocolate donut, and as God is my witness, I'm going to have one! Hey, I like this hands-free phone thing. I can talk, drive, and gesture dramatically."

Amy's laugh crackled through the static. "Okay Scarlett, forget about the Oscar® and put both hands on the wheel."

"Yeah, I think I should. The lady in the next car is giving me a weird look."

"By the way, I thought of another name for the blue beast," Amy said. "How about 'Glacier'?"

"Glacier! Why?"

"It's huge, slow, and the heater never works."

I laughed and patted the steering wheel. "Nah. She deserves a better name than that."

"Okay fine. But after two years, you'd think you would have named her."

1

"A car's name has to be just right. Now hush. I'm going to stop at DW and then I'll be in."

"But, Jen, don't get a donut."

"Amy, don't start n…"

"Get two and make mine maple."

I laughed. "Idiot. I'll be there in ten."

"What?"

"I'll be there in ten."

"Jen, you're breaking up."

"Amy?"

"The reception… town stinks."

"It stinks outside town, too."

"What?"

"Never mind. I'll see you in ten."

"Oh hell. Jen? I'll see you in a few minutes."

"That's what I said."

"What?"

"Bye!" I shouted. I reached down, pushed the phone's end button, and steered the van into the left turn lane at Main Street. I glanced to the right; the rising August sun made me squint. The clear, brilliant light transformed the lampposts and trees into amorphous black silhouettes. When I looked to the left, though, everything was highlighted in perfect detail, each leaf on the trees, each bend in the old wrought iron lampposts. I smiled. The boys and I had watched *Toy Story* the night before I took them up for their two weeks at Katie's. This looked like a scene from it: beautifully lit and almost hyper-realistic. The light also glinted on the front windows of my destination: Donut World. Inside, slanted shelves presented trays of chocolate, maple, sprinkled, raised, and old-fashioned donuts. I couldn't see the cinnamon rolls or the bear claws because of the rather expansive rear ends of a couple of people standing in line. I reached down and pinched the roll of fat hanging over the top of my jeans. "Hello fatness my old friend," I sang softly.

The light clicked to green; I started into the intersection. Movement to the right where there should be no movement. Out of the blinding sun, a speeding blur of brown and rust. The blur became the ugly front end of an uglier sedan going through the red light, heading toward the crosswalk without slowing...

"Jesus H. Christ!" I yelled. I jammed my foot down on the brake pedal.

Can't stop, no way going to stop, going to crash, tearing metal, shattering glass, hospital months, the boys! Who'll take care of the boys! Boys so scared, can't work, lose everything I love them so much I love them so much please please please

The tires grabbed and chittered across the pavement. The van rocked to a stop as the sedan roared past with no more than an inch to spare.

"Oh God," I breathed. "Oh thank you thank you...you...you... son... of... a... bitch!"

I turn to shout more, what I'll never know because the sedan doesn't stop, doesn't slow, just roars on, hits a steel plate in the road left by a construction crew, goes airborne for a brief second, slams back down, tires chirp black rubber on the pavement, trunk pops open, straining against the bungee cords holding it, sun spears into the dark space and highlights...

a small, bare arm, a tiny perfect hand, a shock of blond hair

...trunk lid slams down, black exhaust pulses out of rusted tailpipe.

"No," *I whisper and shake my head.* "No."

An arm.

"No, a doll."

A small sweep of gold hair.

"No, a scarf, or a bag..."

Car recedes down street. Light turns to amber overhead. Diesel pickup truck behind rumbles and ticks. Woman in striped blue dress stands on the corner and stares.

A man's voice floated from the rumbling truck behind me. "It's over now, lady. You can move." I heard his voice but I couldn't quite register it.

Small hand

"What do I do? I... what do I do?" I whispered. My head turned to follow the sedan, but nothing else moved: my hands were locked on the wheel at ten and two; my foot persisted in its attempt to push the brake pedal through the floor.

A horn blasted and I jerked as if I'd touched a live wire.

My eyes flicked up to the rear view. The man in the car behind had his hands raised to his shoulders, palms up. He arched his brows and shrugged.

My leg shook as I let off the brake and touched the accelerator. I oh-so-gingerly steered the van onto Main, past the plate glass windows, the donuts, and the people within, pastries in hand watching as the van passed. The sedan was still visible a couple of blocks ahead…

Shock of hair

…stopped three lights down by a continuous stream of crosswise traffic.

I picked up the phone, and put it back down.

It was a hand. I know it was.

Or anything else, for that matter, idiot. Probably a doll.

It was a hand and blond hair. Strawberry blond.

It was only a second. And from 5 yards, 10, maybe even 15 yards away. In a speeding car. You're crazy!

A little, perfect hand.

I fumbled the cell phone open, and my thumb trembled as it hovered over the nine in indecision. I hit the four instead, followed by two ones.

"Police." I swallowed hard, trying to control the shaking in my voice. "Non-emergency number, please."

"Thank you, we'll connect you."

"Communications," a woman's voice, brisk, efficient.

"Hi," I said and a small, nervous chuckle escaped. "I don't know whether I should have called or not."

"Do you have an emergency?" asked the voice.

"Well, I don't know, really." I slowed and stopped the van behind the line of cars waiting at the light. A steady stream of cars going through the intersection had trapped the sedan at the crosswalk. The sedan's driver revved the engine, rocking the car forward, blowing a cloud of blue-black smoke out the back and over the car behind. Three cars back from the sedan, vestiges of the smoke drifted past my van.

"Perhaps you could call back when you do know," the woman said.

"No, wait! Please. I, well, I was almost in an accident. I mean, I was turning onto Main and this guy in this old car blasted through the intersection and almost hit me."

"Did he hit you?"

"No, but…"

"I'm sorry, but there's really nothing we can do."

"No, that's not why I'm calling!" I swallowed hard, took a deep breath, and noticed my hands were shaking on the steering wheel. I gripped the wheel harder and concentrated on making my voice calm. "Look, do you have any reports of a missing child?"

"Excuse me? What does that have to do with a near accident?"

"I know this probably sounds nuts, but after this guy almost hit my car, he hit a bump in the road, see, and the hood, I mean the trunk, well it was hooked with bungee cords so when he hit the steel plate the trunk lid sort of bounced up for a second and I could have sworn I saw a little kid in there, or at least I think I did, I mean I think I saw a hand."

There was a long pause. "Did you get the license number of the car?"

Damn!

"Uh, no."

"Are you sure of what you saw? It sounds like it happened very fast."

I concentrated, trying to see the trunk slightly open, bungees straining, light stabbing in. Doll? Girl? Nothing? "Well, no."

"Okay, can you describe the car?"

"Well, it's sort of a brown and rust colored sedan, I guess."

"Make? Year?"

"I don't know cars very well."

Another pause. "So, Ma'am, you're almost in an accident and for a split second this trunk opens and you think you see a kidnapping victim in the back of this car."

I felt a burning flush move over my cheeks. "Oh boy, does this sound nuts."

There was another pause and the woman's voice softened. "No, it's always best to call when you think you see something."

The light ahead changed and the rust-colored sedan moved through the intersection and picked up speed. I slowly accelerated away from the light, watching the sedan pulling away. "I know this sounds stupid, but I would have felt really awful if it turned out some little child had been grabbed and I didn't call."

"If it makes you feel any better, there aren't any reports of a child being taken. Look, if you can get the license number, please call back and we'll take it down. I have your number on caller I.D. If a report comes in, we will contact you."

"Okay, thanks."

"Really, it's highly unlikely that you saw anything. Near accidents can be very frightening, and in that highly charged state, your brain can see something totally innocent and twist it into something sinister."

"Okay, thanks. Look, I'm really sorry…"

There was a crackle of static and the sound of urgent voices at the dispatcher's end. "I have to disconnect now."

"Okay, thanks for…" The phone cut off. "…your time." I pressed the end key.

Okay, now I feel stupid.

The brown sedan was three blocks ahead, speeding through a 25-mile-per-hour zone.

But it looked like a hand. And it looked like hair.

I gritted my teeth and accelerated in the wake of the sedan.

At least I can get the license number.

The car and the truck ahead, between me and the sedan, stubbornly refused to realize that I was in the middle of a crisis and remained at 25. The sedan had no such compunction to obey the speed limit and was disappearing ahead. There were any number of streets on which it could turn; I'd never see it again. A bubble of frustration mixed (I'm ashamed to admit) with relief welled up as the sedan grew smaller in the distance.

This is ridiculous, anyway. It was a doll. I just was stressed, imagined it. Besides, I've got to get to work.

Two blocks ahead, in the middle of the block, the sedan's brake lights flashed and my heart jumped. The car slowed, pulled toward the curb, and stopped. The cars ahead slowed as they approached the idling car, and swung wide to miss the cloud of blue-black smoke belching out of the tailpipe. The pickup driver just ahead hit his horn and yelled something, but the sedan's driver didn't react as he stared out his window.

Across the street, a little girl, probably no more than six, dressed in red shorts, a white shirt with red hearts, and a Hello Kitty backpack, walked down the fence toward the gate that would let her into the school. Her thick black hair, hanging almost to her waist, swung back and forth across the pink plastic. It shone in the dappled morning sunlight coming through the elms shading the street. On each third step she took a little skip-jump.

"Oh God," I breathed. I could feel the blood drain from my face, and my hands began a little shaking dance on the steering wheel. I fought to just continue driving, just casually drive past the sedan. I dared a glance at the driver, at his perfectly normal face, a little flushed, a little sweaty but otherwise normal: straight, unexceptional nose; mouth not too big, not too small; ordinary dark brown hair framing it; normal, light-colored eyes. The little girl took another skip. The tip of his tongue came out and licked slowly across his upper lip.

My foot, which had eased off the accelerator as I approached, pressed hard as I passed him. In the van's side mirror I saw the girl grab the fence post and spin through the gate. She skipped and then ran across the playground to the office.

Half a block ahead I pulled over to the curb, keeping an eye on the sedan as it slowly drove away from the school and eased up the street. As the sedan passed, I brought my hand up next to my face, pushing at the phone's ear piece with one trembling finger, too frightened to look over and get another look at the man behind the wheel.

The phone rang and I screamed out loud. My hand shook as I pressed the ear bud.

"Hello!"

"Jenny? Hey! How's it going?"

"Jesus, Katie!"

"What?"

"Uh, nothing, nothing." I pulled the van out and started carefully after the sedan. "How are the boys? Are they, uh, are they behaving themselves?"

"They're fine. They miss you. You sound funny."

"Yeah hilarious."

"Something wrong?"

"Yes... "

Katie: loving sister and drama queen…

"…no. It's too hard to explain right now."

"Oh my God, they didn't change Danny's adoption date, did they?"

"No. No! Nothing like that."

"Then what is it?"

"Nothing. I'll tell you later."

"Jennifer." I could hear Katie walking away from the sound of the boys fighting over who was going to be Spiderman and who was going to be Batman. "You're sort of scaring me," she whispered.

"Oh for… Katie, give it a rest. I gotta go. Thanks for taking the boys. You all have fun."

"Hey!"

"Give them a big hug and a kiss and tell them I'll call later, okay? Love you! Bye."

"Jenny…"

I hit the end key.

The phone rang. "Hello?"

"Jennifer, don't you hang up on me! What the hell is going on?"

"Nothing! Katie, I'm driving. I can't talk. I'll call you later. Bye."

"Jenny! You sound like you did last time!"

I listened to three hundred miles of static. "What is that supposed to mean?" I said softly.

"When… when you were fourteen."

"That was 20 years ago!" I shouted. "Christ Almighty! Are you ever going to let that go?"

There was a crackle of static then Katie's two words cut through clearly. She might as well have been sitting next to me. "Are you?"

I tried to focus on the road, breathing deeply. "I don't need this right now. You have no idea how much I don't need this right now. I really have to hang up, Katie. I'm driving. Really, there is nothing going on. I've got to get to work."

"Jenny…"

"Bye, Katie."

When the phone rang again, I hit the end key again, blindly. My eyes were fixed on the brown and rust sedan's trunk as it reached the place where Main Street became Highway 28 and left town.

CHAPTER 2

As the highway went from four lanes to two, a truck and an old VW bug moved over between me and the sedan. By swerving slightly, I could just see the rusted chrome trim around the left taillight of the sedan.

The phone rang again. "God, Katie! Enough!" I patted at the cup holder, fumbled the phone out, and hit the end key as I strained to maintain eye contact with the sedan. He was no longer speeding, maybe because the blue puffs coming out the rusting tailpipe were becoming alarmingly darker and larger as he accelerated.

Okay, I can't let him know he's being followed, but I have to keep him in sight. God, why do I have to be driving a big, frigging, baby blue van? Why didn't I get his license number in town, at the school?

> *Because when you saw him looking at that little girl, your bowels turned to water and you heart started going about 200 beats a minute, that's why.*

"Okay, okay. Now what?"

Get the license number and call the lady back.

The phone rang again. I pushed the button on the ear piece. "Damn it Katie! Stop!"

There was a burst of static, then, "Jeez, what are you fighting with Katie about?" said Amy. "And why aren't... at work and where's ... maple bar?"

"I didn't get the donuts..."

9

"What? Torture… torturing me!"

"Amy…"

"Make …. stupid diet, then tempt… donuts, then yank them away."

"Amy, shut up!"

"What?"

"I said, shut up! I'm losing the signal and I've got to tell you something."

"You're breaking up."

"I know, damn it! Can you hear me?"

"…some."

"Listen carefully, please!"

"You're clear now. Go ahead."

"I had an accident, I mean, almost and I saw something and I'm following a car because I think there's a little girl in the trunk of the car."

There was a long, static-filled pause. "Jen, I know you like practical jokes but this isn't funny."

"I'm not trying to be funny!" I screamed.

"Hey!"

"Sorry, sorry." I took a deep breath and tried to stop the shakes that were causing the steering wheel to twitch back and forth, threatening to send the van crashing through the ditch edging the road and into the wheat field beyond. "I'm scared shitless. I don't know what I'm doing."

"Jen, are you sure you saw something?"

"Of course I'm not sure. It happened really fast."

"Did… call the police?"

"Yes. They didn't believe me."

There was another static-filled pause. "Could you… imagined? I mean, you know because…"

"Because what?" I said slowly.

Another static-filled pause.

"Nothing. But, you might… seen anything."

"Of course I could have! But I can't take the chance."

"…think you imag..?"

"No, no! You're breaking up. Call the police, Amy. Call the police. Tell them we're just passing County Road 42 on 28."

"…County Road 28?"

"No!" I shouted. "Not County Road 28. Highway 28!"

"Wha…?"

"Amy?"

"Amy?"

"…call … police."

"I told you! I did! They didn't believe me! Or are you saying you'll call? Amy? It's Highway 28, Amy. Can you hear me?" There was no response other than the dead silence of a dropped call. I hit send twice to redial, but nothing happened. "Shit!" I came very close to slamming the phone through the dashboard, but instead dropped it shakily back into the cup holder.

Twenty freaking years and they want to make it the defining time of my life! One breakdown… it's not like there wasn't a reason!

I realized I was twisting my hands around the steering wheel tightly enough to make my skin squeak against the plastic cover.

I relaxed them. No problem.

And I hadn't started rubbing the scars on my wrist. Didn't even touch them.

The sedan still farted its way down the road, and more cars were beginning to back up behind my van. The highway stretched out ahead toward the foothills.

Okay, he might be heading to the freeway. I can still follow him on the freeway. He won't see me.

The sedan approached the intersection of one of the county roads, and for a heart-stopping second, I thought he was slowing for the turn, but then another black puff rose in the air and the sedan continued on. As I passed the intersection, I looked down that long, straight empty road and shuddered.

I follow him for a mile or two and then his car suddenly slews across the road, the car door is flung open, and he leaps from the seat holding a gun the size of a cannon. I try to stop, try to turn the van on the narrow road and he grins at me, points the gun, his finger on the trigger…

I shook my head back and forth vigorously, but the image wouldn't dislodge. My foot eased off the accelerator and the speedometer needle began a slow swing to the left.

What the hell am I doing? I'll get myself killed. I can't save that little girl. I can't handle this! Maybe Katie and Amy are right to be worried.

The cars started to pull farther ahead of me, the sedan leading them in a cloud of blue-gray exhaust.

I've got kids to worry about. There probably wasn't even anything in the trunk. It's my stupid imagination. A kid in a trunk? She said there was no kid reported missing. If a kid were missing, someone would have reported it.

Five car lengths separated my van from the short line of cars, then six car lengths, then ten. Almost involuntarily, the van started easing to the side of the road.

Stupid, stupid, stupid. I'm just going to end up making a fool of myself and probably get sued by some poor, innocent stranger. He was just some regular guy…

…except the way he watched that little girl skipping to school; the way his tongue came out and ran across his lip.

As the van slowed, I closed my eyes, just for a second.

A shaft of light, a small arm, a shock of yellow hair.

I tromped down on the accelerator and barely heard the blare of horns as I jammed back into traffic and caught up with the cars ahead. Behind the sedan a VW bug popped along followed by a big green pickup, two SUVs and my big old van…

Blue Moose. Nah. Blue Whale. No.

The phone rang and I nearly drove the van into a call box sign. I pushed the ear bud three times before I could get it to answer the phone.

"Amy?"

"Ms. Canfield?"

"What?"

"This phone number …. Jennifer Canfield. Is that you?"

I recognized the voice, even through the static. My fear, which I'd thought was ratcheted up as high as could be, tripped up several more levels to stark terror. "Yes."

"… County Dispatch. …about 10 minutes ago?"

"Did I call you? Yes, yes, I did. Listen, I think it's real, I truly do…"

The voice mixed with static interrupted. I pressed the earpiece but I couldn't decipher any of the words.

"Why are you calling me? Is there a child missing? Was I right?"

"Where…?"

I strained to hear the words through the broken static.

It must be real. There must be a child missing. Why else would they call? Because they think I'm a nut job?

What did Amy tell them?

It doesn't matter. I know what I saw…

…do you?

"Yes, I do," I muttered. "Are you asking what direction he went?" I said loudly. "West. He's going west. I'm following him."

"…following?"

"Yes, I'm following. I'm on 28."

"…28…where?" The static was worse, the words barely audible. I pushed on the ear button until it started a dull throbbing in my ear.

"Highway 28! We're going west on Highway 28!"

Static.

"Did you hear me?"

Static, then dead silence.

"Shit, shit, shit! Stinking, lousy, miserable cell phones!" This time I did slam the phone down.

Why did I have to see that stinking car? Why couldn't I have fucking blinked! I don't want to do this!

Oh, and that little girl asked to be in that trunk? Stop whining!

"Well, it's her fault," I said out loud, and then stopped, shocked, wanting to look around to see who'd said those words, knowing that it was me, and almost hearing the words that should have/could have followed:

Just like it was your fault.

"Stop," I whispered. "We are *not* going there."

CHAPTER 3

The line of cars stopped at the stoplight just before the freeway over-crossing. A couple of cars peeled off on 240 heading north. There were only two cars now between me and the sedan. The van idled in the line of cars and I looked off to the right. The exit ramp there led onto the freeway. It was the entrance I used when I was going up to visit Katie and Jon, the entrance I'd taken just a few days ago when I'd driven the boys up for their two weeks in the mountains with Aunt Katie and Uncle Jon. The freeway stretched out straight through hay fields then rose through the rolling brown hills beyond. Very little traffic was on it at this time of day. It looked peaceful.

It'd be easy to bear to the right, enter that straight stretch of road, blow off work and head north, just cruise on up that freeway and see the boys because there really had been nothing in that trunk...

I shook my head once, sharply.

I didn't imagine it.

Katie's voice: "You sound like you did last time."

Christ! She acts like what happened to me was some sort of fantasy, like what he did...

Shook my head. Remembered my therapist's voice gently saying, It's not happening now. This is old.

It's been 20 years. I don't even think about... him anymore.

Oh, is that why you date so much?

"Shut up," I whispered.

The light changed and I followed the line of cars over the overpass toward the mountains. The hills, brown with dark-green blotches, had been a verdant green a few months before. The manzanita and the coastal oaks in the folds of the hills were still green, but the wild grasses that had grown over the open spaces had died quickly under the California summer sun. The brilliant morning light made the brown grass look like gold on the ridges. An unusually clear blue sky rose above the hills. A breeze overnight had cleared away the smog.

The sedan continued at its steady pace, heading toward the gap in the hills cut by Landerson Creek. The highway followed the creek's path on its way down from Stanton Lake. As we approached the hills I kept glancing at my phone, praying to see a few bars, but not one even flickered on the indicator.

They'll figure out it's Highway 28. Of course they will. They must have a report of a missing child; that's why they called me. In the meantime, all I have to do is drive.

The cars turned into the small town of Camilla. The highway doubled as the main route through town and passed the high school and the library. Kids were just starting to appear, but the mad rush of parents' cars hadn't started yet. A trio of kids tripped up the sidewalk, three boys with oversized t-shirts and sagging pants. I stared at them as I went past, willing them to understand that I was in terrible trouble, that I needed help. One of them met my gaze, a young man with long black hair and large, deep-set, kind-looking eyes. Our eyes locked for just a second, and I started to call something out the window, I don't know what, when he lifted a one-finger salute. "Take a picture next time," he shouted, "it'll last longer." The three broke into raucous laughter. I bit my lower lip and faced forward again as their laughter faded quickly behind me.

The road took a left turn and headed out into orchards and farmland as it approached the first foothills.

Any minute now. Any minute.

I kept glancing in the rearview mirror.

Any second now, flashing lights, and cars moving over to the right and I can move over to the right and let the professionals take it.

Behind me were two cars, a black Jeep, winding road, and lots of trees. No blue lights. No red lights.

It truly was a lovely day to be driving up the valley. The hills covered with brush and golden brown grass provided a backdrop for the lush green of the almond and walnut orchards. The hills rose on each side of the valley cut by the creek as we turned north and traveled further away from home and safety. Normally, it was one of my favorite drives. Only two weeks ago I'd brought the boys up the valley to play in Landerson Creek, skipping stones and looking for bugs, splashing in the water until their fingers were like prunes. Richie had found a frog, Danny a cricket.

Oh God, I want it to be then! I want to be with my boys. I want the sun to be shining and the birds to be singing and have all right with the world.

The caravan of cars rounded several more bends and passed homes and ranches. The clock on the dashboard clicked away the minutes and still there was no sign of the law.

They went to County Road 28. Damn it! Stinking, lousy phones!

The line of cars had built behind me. We all went through a long dip and came through some trees into a wider, more developed area. The driver in the car in front of me turned on his right turn signal. Then I noticed that all the cars in front and behind me were turning on their signals and heading for an exit, all of them except for the sedan.

"Oh shit," I whispered.

The Landerson Creek Casino loomed on the hillside on the right: a mammoth complex of casino, resort, parking garages, and acres of parking lots. As the cars started peeling off, it was everything I could do not to follow them.

I could go in and tell someone. They could call the police. That would be best, best for everyone. He'll keep going up the highway. They'll find him. There's nowhere else to go.

Except the dozens of side roads where he could disappear…

I watched the blue smoke still farting out of the rusting tailpipe, the sun beating down on the trunk lid, and I could *see* a little child lying in there, whimpering, terrified, and still it took every bit of strength I had to keep the wheel straight, to continue up the highway past the signs promising luck and money, not to go in where there were lots of people, and a phone to call the police who would take this burden, this drowning fear.

Okay, the van might have wavered a little, but it didn't slow. I stared at the trunk lid. "I'm not going to leave you, little one," I whispered. I dropped back as far as I dared, terrified that I'd lose him.

Terrified I wouldn't.

We drove past hayfields and orchards, pastures dotted with cows and horses, open land bordered at the back with trees marking the path of the creek. After several miles, the valley walls started coming together, becoming more of a canyon than a valley. The rocky outcrops along the road were dotted with brilliant orange poppies. Above, farmland was now steep hillsides spotted with dusty green manzanita, scrub brush, and oak trees; above them taller hills were covered with a mixture of oaks and evergreens. The hot smell of sage and pine wafted through the window on the warm breeze. The road came alongside the creek again and I caught glimpses of long stretches of sparkling water tumbling over the rocks.

A dusty-red new Mustang convertible appeared on a rise behind me. It came up quickly, driven by a blonde in big sunglasses with a multicolored scarf holding her long hair back.

I could wave her down… and then what?

Instead, I swung into the first pullout I saw, and let the blonde pass me. The woman gave me a nice little wave then accelerated up the hill. I pulled back out and eased ahead, just catching a glimpse of the sedan ahead of the Mustang as it rose up a hill and disappeared around a bend at the top.

"Okay," I whispered to myself as I followed them up the hill. "A couple more cars between and maybe he won't spot… Blue Beulah. No… Blue… oh, shit."

Just over the rise a large electronic sign on the right shoulder blinked out its message: One Way Traffic Ahead; Prepare To Stop. Past the sign in a large gravel turnout, a truck was parked, three men in white hardhats leaning over the hood, looking at something on a large piece of paper. Their truck was parked to the side of a long straight stretch of road where a dozen cars sat in the sun. At the end of the line sat the red Mustang, and just ahead of it, the battered sedan, still puffing its evil blue smoke. At the base of the hill, at the front of the line of cars, a worker stood, legs straddling the yellow line, a stop sign in her hand. Beyond the stop sign was empty road, no sign of what was causing the closure, just two empty lanes curving around a cliff and disappearing.

I coasted up behind the Mustang, thinking furiously.

If I try to signal those guys, he'll see me and take off. By the time I get them to understand, he'll be back up the road off on a side route and he'll never be found. Or, what if he has a gun and starts shooting everyone, starting with that sweet baby in the trunk? Think, Jen, think!

I pasted a big smile on my face, pushed the door of the van open and stepped out on the hot pavement. I started around the front of the van, supremely conscious of the blonde's eyes watching me in her rearview mirror, knowing that the sedan's driver could be doing the same. I waved at the men standing by the truck. "Hello!"

They looked up from the papers spread on the hood. All had white hardhats with some sort of red symbol on the front. They were all deeply tanned, and though they in no way looked the same, they all wore the same wary expression. The tallest, a big bear of a guy with black shaggy hair, cleared his throat. "Ma'am, the traffic will move again in a minute," he called. "It's not going to be a long delay."

"No," I said, trying for gaiety but achieving something just short of hysteria, "that's not it, I'm completely lost. Can one of you nice gentlemen give me directions?" I kept walking toward them, refusing to look at the sedan. "They told me to get on 28 and just keep going, but it seems like I've been on here for at least two days now, and I haven't seen a sign for Stanton Lake, just some casino back there." My voice was wildly energetic. I concentrated on the man who'd spoken. A flicker crossed his face.

Don't worry, mister. I'm not crazy. Just scared shitless.

He glanced at the two other guys, then took a step toward me. "Ma'am, you should get back in your van. The pilot car will be through any minute."

"Okay, yeah, sure, no problem, but I really am lost so can you give me directions?"

He looked back at the other two men, shrugged as if to say, let me take care of the crazy fat lady and we can get back to work. "Why don't you get back in your car in case the traffic starts?"

"Sure, sure, no problem."

He followed me around the front of the car and when I climbed back in, he pushed the door closed, then rested his hands on the window frame. His hands were big enough that they seemed to cover half the opening. He gave me a 100-watt, I'm-the-most-charming-guy-you'll-ever-meet-so-let's-get-this-over-with-quickly smile.

"Where are you going?" he asked.

I tried to keep the smile on my face, the smile that if the guy in the sedan saw it would think, oh, she's just a harmless dingbat asking directions. "Well, if it's true about good intentions, I'm going straight to hell."

He blinked. "Excuse me?"

I took a deep breath. "You're going to think I'm crazy but you're just going to have to believe me. The car two cars ahead—no, don't look!—it's an old sedan, and it's being driven by a kidnapper, and he has a little girl in the trunk."

The man's smile faded and he started to push back. I reached over and grabbed his hand, then quickly released it when he flinched. "No, please, no, you've got to believe me. I'm not making this up. I called the police but I lost the phone signal but they called back and I think they called because a child had been taken but I kept losing the signal..." My smile stayed stretched across my face but the tears were starting to spill from my eyes. "I saw something, in his trunk, and yes, I could be wrong, but I don't think so, and I can't take the chance, so, please, does your phone work? Can you call the police? When you go back over to your truck, can you try to see his license and tell them? I'm trying to follow him but I'm terrified and if he sees me he'll take off and I'll lose him and that little girl...I mean I don't know if it's a little girl but I think it is with strawberry blonde hair..." A sob took the last word, but I fought to keep the smile, the pretense of just asking directions, just a few simple directions.

He stared at me for a long moment, and then he lifted one arm and pointed ahead. "Yeah," he said loudly. "Just keep following this road another 10 miles or so and you'll run into Highway 9. Go left and that'll take you to Stanton Lake."

"Please, please believe me."

"Okay, then," he said and slapped his hands against the door. "You have a safe drive."

I tried to smile.

He believed me. That's why he played along.

He walked between the van and the Mustang, tapped twice on the van's hood and gave me a thumbs up. He smiled, winked, went back to the other two men, spoke for several seconds, and the three men burst out laughing.

The brief upwelling of relief washed away in a flood of despair as the laughter echoed across the road. I stared ahead, trying to stop the tears, trying to think as the minutes ticked by. Then I saw the construction company's pilot car appear around the cliff down the road, leading a line of southbound cars and I knew my time was up. The drivers ahead of me started swinging car doors shut. Those who had cut their engines restarted them. The pilot car swung around in a circle coming to a stop in front of our northbound cars. The southbound cars accelerated up the lane past us and I watched each of them flit by and disappear.

I've come this far, I can keep on going. The police have to come, they have to.

There was a sharp rap on the passenger window and I flinched like I'd been shot. The tall construction worker stood on the other side smiling and spinning his finger in a loop. "Open the window," he mouthed.

I pushed the button.

He smiled his hundred-watt smile again as the glass lowered. "Listen, I know it's an imposition, but if you're going to Stanton Lake, could you give me a ride?"

"I…"

He smiled, if possible, even brighter. "It sure would save me a lot of time and trouble, if you don't mind." He took his hardhat off, reached for the door handle, nodded and raised a hand at his companions back at the truck. "She said yes," he called. "I'll see you guys later."

He slid into the seat and dropped his hat on the floor behind. He reached for the seat belt.

I stared at him. "I thought…"

"The cars are going," he said, clicking the belt and nodding at the line of cars starting out ahead of them.

"I saw you laughing," I said. "I thought you didn't believe…"

He waved at the cars ahead. "Go! Quickly! And smile."

I forced a smile, put the van in gear, and then wiped at the wetness on my face while trying to look like I wasn't wiping at the wetness on my face.

"To tell you the truth," he said, "I didn't believe you. You've got to admit that's a pretty wild story."

I accelerated, bringing the car into line with the others following slowly behind the pilot car.

"But," he said, "I figured it wouldn't kill me to make a call."

"Your cell phone works?"

"No, but the CB does. Bob got the sedan's plate number and I called the office. There's an Amber alert out for a missing 4-year-old girl. They're calling the sheriff and the highway patrol and, as far as I know, the Marines, right now. And, I figured you might need some company so I hitched a ride."

I took another deep, shuddering breath and started to cry again.

He looked at me, worried. "Oh, now, don't do that."

I blinked hard, trying to see the cars ahead through the blur of tears. "I didn't know, you see, I thought I saw something, but I wasn't sure, and I've been driving up this road, following him, and tissue."

He looked startled. "What?"

I gestured wildly at the floor at his feet and sniffed. "Tissue, I need a tissue," I sobbed. "I kept thinking that I was just making a total fool of myself, but I couldn't let it go, I just kept thinking that if it was true, and I didn't try to do something, I'd never be able, be able… under the backpack. There's a box."

"What? Oh." He shoved aside a sweatshirt and a couple of CDs; underneath was a backpack and under that the remnant of a squashed tissue box with a few crumpled tissues hanging out. "This is a box?"

"Just hand me the tissue." He lifted the box toward me and I plucked a tissue out and wiped at my face.

"Let me guess," he said looking down at the Iron Man emblazoned in red and black on the backpack. "You have children."

"You're psychic," I said and blew my nose one-handed.

"I'm going to go one step farther." He twisted around and he looked over into the back of the van at the two basketballs, Spiderman sweatshirt, scattering of Matchbox cars, child's car seat, booster seat, and various pieces of several different plastic aircraft. "They're boys."

"Positively amazing."

"How many, six?"

"Just two."

"Hmmm. You're sure?"

"Yes." I grinned and rubbed at my nose with the tissue one last time. I took a couple of slow, deep breaths and let each out with a sigh. "Thanks," I said. "You really called the police?"

"No," he said. "I called Pizza Guys. Pepperoni, mushroom, and sausage, right?"

"They're really coming?"

"Thirty minutes or less."

"Oh shut up." I grinned at him. "This will be over soon, won't it? And that little girl will be safe."

"Indubitably. So, it's the brown P.O.S. two cars up?"

"Yeah."

He leaned outward, staring past the Mustang. "A P.O.S. driven by a P.O.S."

He looked at me and the cold anger in his black eyes made me blink, but then he smiled again. "Putting aside the swollen eyes, running nose, and the van that looks like a toy store, two McDonald's and a Taco Bell threw up in it, you look fairly normal. How'd you get into this?"

"Putting aside the oh so subtle insult in that question…" I took a deep, hitching breath and let it out with a whoosh. "Well, I was on the way to work…" I told him in detail what had happened, the near accident, the glimpse inside the dark trunk and the searing sight of that tiny hand and golden hair. I brought him up right to the point where I'd heard him laughing with the other men before my voice quit.

"So, anyway," I said after a moment, "my boss always said donuts would be the death of me, but I didn't really think she meant literally."

"Donuts, hmmm."

"Yes, donuts."

"Do you know," he said, looking over at me, "you may be the first woman I've ever met who has actually admitted eating donuts?"

23

"Hey," I said as if insulted, gesturing down at the oversized shirt I wore, the roll hanging over the waistband of the stretch jeans. "I didn't get this way by running around eating carrot sticks."

He stared at me for a second, startled, and then a great bray of laughter burst out. "I shouldn't be laughing," he said, "we're in a serious situation here." But he was still chuckling when the pilot car at the head of the line came to the end of the construction zone and began its u-turn to take its place at the head of the line of southbound cars.

As soon as the pilot moved over, the cars ahead of us accelerated rapidly up the grade. The sedan couldn't keep up and fell behind the pack, the tailpipe's belching increasing until the red Mustang behind it was traveling in a blue-grey cloud. The blonde made frantic waving motions in front of her face, and then, fed up with the smoke and the delay, took a dangerous chance on a blind curve and passed the sedan with one finger raised.

"Now what?"

"Just what we're doing. The sheriff has got to be here any minute."

"We're the only car behind him. It's not likely he's missed us."

Not this Big Bird. Big Blue Bird.

No, definitely not.

"It'll be okay."

"How is it going to be okay?"

"So," he said, pointedly ignoring my question. "Your husband know where you are?"

I looked over at him, startled. "I'm not married."

"Well, you know, woman, children, usually there's a man somewhere in the mix."

I felt my face heat up. "Uh... no man."

"Woman?"

"No. I'm single. I mean, if I were married, it would be a man, but I..." I shut my mouth and stared at the road.

After a moment: "So, what'd you think when you heard that knock on the window and this tall, magnificent stranger talked his way into your car?"

I turned and gawked at him. He smiled, shrugged, and lifted his hands, gesturing down at himself.

I laughed. "Truth? I wondered if you were going to fit in that seat."

"Yeah, this woman I once dated used to say that I didn't get in a car; I put one on."

"Even this big blue…"

Beelzebub? Yuck! No.

"…van looked like it was going to be a tight fit."

"What was that?"

"Oh, it's silly. A game I've had for the last few years, trying to think of a name… Oh shit!"

"What?"

The brake lights on the sedan flashed, then stayed red as the sedan slowed. "He's turning! He's turning off the road!"

The sedan pulled to the right, bumping over broken asphalt and pits filled with road debris and mud, then it turned into a narrow road bordered on each side by scrub and trees and disappeared.

"How am I going to follow him?" I said. "He'll see us!"

"Calm down! Just take a breath."

"You take a breath!" I looked in the rear view mirror, and the side mirrors. No cars in sight, no houses nearby.

"Go past," he said.

"What? I am not leaving her!"

"No, no, just go past. Act normal. He might be watching to see if we slow down or turn. Just do it!"

He stared straight ahead and I forced myself to do the same as we passed the narrow drive.

"I'm going to stop," I said, just as he said, "Pull up here."

We stared at each other. "Still no phone?" he asked.

I glanced down. "Not a single blessed bar." I looked up, gasped, and reached for the door handle. "There's a car coming. I'm going to flag them down."

"Good! Great!"

I jumped out and started waving frantically at the maroon PT Cruiser heading toward us. For just a moment I actually thought they were stopping, I know the young man behind the wheel saw me, but instead of slowing he stomped on the gas and raced around the next bend with a faint squeal of tires.

"Chicken-shit son-of-a-bitch bleeding bastard!"

"No, don't hold it in. Tell me what you really think."

"Cowardly little…" We both looked up and down the road.

"We can't wait," I said softly.

"I know," he said. "I've been on this road for two weeks. Not going to be much traffic this time of day from the lake. And the cycle on the pilot car averages six and a half minutes, so nobody from the south for at least that long.

"We could lose him," I said.

"Yeah we could."

We looked at each other and then we got back in the van. I backed it up and then turned carefully up the narrow road.

CHAPTER 4

Calling that narrow lane a road was giving it more honor than it was due. Thin, broken asphalt crumbled under the tires and long neglected tree branches dragged across the windows, screeching and snapping against the trim. As insignificant as the road appeared, however, it came out of the trees to a good-sized steel bridge spanning Landerson Creek. I slowed the van and peered across the bridge. There was no sign of the sedan.

"Damn! We didn't miss a turnoff, did we?" I asked.

"No, I'm sure of it," he said. "He must have gone across."

I eased the van out and bumped over the bridge, waiting for the otherwise solid looking steel structure to collapse beneath us. With nary a split nor tremor, we made it to the other side and stopped dead where the road split east and south, the south portion following back down the creek in the direction we'd come, the eastward portion climbing up into the hills and disappearing around a limestone outcropping.

"Which way?"

"Let me look," he said and flung open the passenger door. He ran a little way east, stared at the ground, reached down and touched something, then jogged south along the creek. He turned and ran to the van. "East... left," he said as he dropped back in the seat.

I swung the van east and followed the dirt road up into the scrub and rock strewn foothills. "Yes, kemosabe."

He looked at me, startled. "Do you always whistle in graveyards?"

"Every time," I said. "You should see me at funerals. I'm a real hoot."

"There's nothing wrong with laughing at fear," he said.

"Well then watch out, cause I'm about to laugh up the storm of the century."

"So you're scared?"

"Terrified. You?"

"My mouth is so dry you could strike a match," he said.

I stared up the dirt road, trying to see around the curves, trying to get a glimpse of that dirty brown car as the van bounced over the ruts. We came around the limestone outcropping, but there was still no sign of the sedan.

I swerved around a hole. "I just want her to be okay," I said softly, almost involuntarily. "If we get there too late... I mean, if that animal... She can't be hurt like that. No one, ever, should be hurt like that. People think if kids get away they're okay, but they aren't. Not if he... If he does..."

"We won't be late," he said and reached over and squeezed my hand on the steering wheel...

...and his hand was warm, the skin rough and callused and...

I flinched and jerked my hand away. I tried to ease the motion into a rub of my neck, but the van hit a rock and I had to grip the wheel again, tightly. "You're sure this is the right way?" I said, not looking at him.

"Pretty sure. It looked like the tire tracks going this way were fresh." He looked over at me. "Sorry if I startled you."

"You didn't."

Liar.

The van bounced through a couple of ruts causing the toys in the back to clatter against each other. I cranked the wheel and brought the van through a tight turn and we started climbing higher into the hills.

"I'm not some sort of creep, or anything," he said.

"Oh, no, I know. Just a uh... neck spasm."

We jerked and bounced up the uneven, rocky road.

"There's dust in the air," he said after several seconds. "He had to have come this way. You can see it in the air. The sunlight's reflecting off it."

"You're right! We must be on the right road. Which means, that he's ahead of us which means we'd better figure out what the hell we're going to do."

"Yeah, I know. I've been thinking about that. We can't count on the sheriff to find us. They're looking on the highway and I don't think they're going to see that little turnoff. And," he said, "if he's turned off on this road, it's either because he thinks he's being followed, or this is where he's going to, uh, to..."

"Okay. No need to spell it out."

No need to explain it to me.

"So a plan, a plan." He ran his hands back through his black hair and scrubbed at his scalp. "You know, I can design a road, fix a road, do anything you want with asphalt and concrete. But what the hell do I know about this? What do we do if we screw up and get this little girl killed? Or ourselves? Put me behind the wheel of a bulldozer and I can do anything, but I don't have the faintest damn idea how to handle this."

"Hey, Mr. Cool." I looked over at him, back at the windshield, then over at him again. "Don't lose it now." I swerved around a monstrous rut and splashed the van through a trickle of water that came off the hillside, crossed the road, and tumbled down some rocks on the other side.

He sighed and shook his head. "Mr. Cool. Yeah right. Out on the highway, this seemed like a game," he said, "a great story to tell. Rescuing the lovely lady in distress, saving a little girl, the sheriff arriving in the nick of time." He sighed. "When we headed over that bridge, and up this road, it started becoming a little too real." He clutched at the arm rest and braced his hand flat against the ceiling as we went over a particularly bad bump. "I have all the respect in the world for sheriff's deputies, especially the ones in this county, but how the hell are they going to find us up here?"

I looked over at him, then back at the road, dodging the bad bumps, easing over the ruts. "The only thing we can do," I said, "is the best we can."

Though I kept my eyes on the road, I could tell that he stared at me for a long moment. "You're right," he said. His voice was back down to the low gravelly pitch that I'd first heard back on the road.

"We can't go back," I said. "There's no way I'm leaving that little girl."

"No," he said, "we sure as hell can't go back. But oh my god, I'd give my left... ear to be still standing back at the truck bullshitting with the guys."

I snorted, trying to laugh, not quite making it. "Ear."

"Or words to that effect." He tried to smile, but it was a pretty weak attempt.

We were going through a patch of oaks, but the way ahead opened back up into sunshine. The narrow road had been cut into the south-facing curve of a grass-covered hill dotted with a few scrub oaks and some rough, gray boulders. Steep hillside on one side, sheer drop on the other. It followed the contour up to a pass at the top where a lone pine stood, clinging to the outer edge of the road. The sun was heading toward mid-morning and cast a black shadow from the pine across the road, the boulders, and hill. The shadow also lay across a car.

"So that plan," I said, my voice rising, "I hope you've got one because I see his car."

Next to the pine, the brown sedan sat, halfway in the road, steam rising around the hood and dissolving into the branches above. The driver stood near the right taillight in the shade of the pine. The tree looked as if at any moment it would lose its grip on the crumbling hillside and go tumbling down the ravine.

Go tree, go! And take him with you!

His arms were crossed and he was staring down at us.

"Holy shit," the man beside me breathed.

"What do we do?"

"Just keep going."

"Are you insane?"

"Probably, but if we stop, he'll know something's wrong."

"Like he doesn't already."

"You don't know that!"

"Oh shit oh shit oh shit oh shit."

30

As we came closer, I took in his outfit: black t-shirt, black jeans, even his shoes were black—high top Converses that looked like they'd been used hard. He was tall and looked like he worked outdoors at some job that kept him strong. Wiry muscles flexed in his forearms. A huge tattoo snaked up his right arm. As we got closer, I saw that rather than a reptile, it was one word elaborately worked: Badass.

Oh, and he thinks he looks like one, doesn't he? A real tough man, who picks on little girls. Bastard! Cowardly bastard.

Fear turned to a burning anger. I glanced at the man beside me. He looked three times as big as Badass and the look in his eyes and the set of his jaw...

Badass just might find out what that word really means.

The sedan driver didn't move. Only his eyes followed us as I slowed the car to a stop and bared my teeth at him in an attempt at a smile. His face was stony, but I could see the glisten of sweat dripping down from his right temple.

"Ask him directions," I said.

His eyebrows went up. "Directions? Directions. Right. Uh, no, on second thought... I know. Just stay put." He got out of the car and stretched. "Hey," he called. "Having trouble?"

The man stared at him for a long minute. "Some," he finally said. Despite his tough guy pose, his voice trembled slightly. His eyes kept shifting from the tall construction worker to me behind the wheel. That tremor in his voice raised goose bumps on my arms in spite of the heat.

"Want some help?"

"No," the guy said. He shook his head. "You should get on out of here. This here's a private road."

"Oh, no, I don't think so." The construction worker turned back to the car. "Hey... Ellen. This is a public road, right?"

Ellen? I look like an Ellen?

I rolled down my window and leaned out. "It is if we're on the right road. Ask him," I called.

"What?"

"Ask him where we are!"

"I know where we are."

"Samuel Clemens St. John," I said. "You have no idea where you are and you know it. Ask him directions."

He looked back at me and his eyes widened then he walked slowly toward the driver. "Well, I might be a little lost." As he walked closer to the sedan's driver, the man began to back toward the tree. His arms were still crossed in front of him. He kept looking back and forth at the two of us and the sweat was now dripping down the sides of his face. "The map showed this road like it was a regular road and then we go bumping over some antique bridge and up into the hills, and well, it's getting a little like the beginning of some horror movie."

"I… I s…seen you down on the road," the man said.

"Did you? Yeah, we were behind you and then we saw you turn on this road and I told Ellen, there, that must be the road."

"You followed me," the man said.

"Samuel" gave him his 100-watt smile. "Well, sort of, but just because I thought you knew where you were going. Stupid me."

I looked at "Samuel." I could see him starting to relax, becoming more confident as he faced the sweating, trembling man.

I eased my door open and stepped down onto the hot dirt road and walked slowly toward the sedan. It was still morning, but the sun streaming from the east seemed unnaturally hot. I could feel pinpricks of sweat starting out down my arms and back.

"I don't like people following me." His voice rose. He was shaking.

"Sir, we certainly didn't mean to follow you and I don't know quite how we got on this godforsaken road, but if you can just tell us how to find our way out, we'll get out of your hair." As he talked, I came up to the car and stood near the left taillight, facing Badass. He stood up against the right taillight, his arms still tightly crossed, which seemed odd considering the sweat darkening his t-shirt. Samuel stood nearer the van, forming the apex of our tense little triangle. Badass flicked his eyes at me, then back to Samuel.

"I don't like people following me!" he said again, louder.

Samuel glanced over at me, a small smile on his face.

I frowned at him and shook my head slightly.

Samuel took a step toward the other man, and the man began to uncross his arms and his left hand had a gun in it, black, the sun glinting off the short barrel. The gun shook but still rose toward

Samuel, and the anger inside me—which had started when I'd seen that tattoo—surged up through me like a blast cloud.

"Oh, no fucking way!" I shouted, my voice starting as a growl and ending as a shout. I launched at Badass, focusing on the hand clutching the gun, thinking frantically,

Push it up! Push it up!

I grabbed his wrist with both hands and pushed skyward and the gun went off with an unbelievable explosion of noise. Samuel ducked under it and drove a punch into the center of that black t-shirt and the man's breath blew out in a grunt. Gripping his wrist was like holding onto steel. The man may have been a coward, but he was a strong coward and his panic made him even stronger. He pulled and I clutched with both hands, clinging with all my strength as he jerked me back and forth, trying to shake me loose. He swung his other arm out, slamming it across Samuel's chest, driving him back a step. He pulled his gun hand down, I felt his wrist flex and the gun went off again. Samuel dropped into the dirt and the bullet passed harmlessly over him and struck the road just past the van. He was too strong, I knew I couldn't hold him, so I brought my mouth down and bit the bastard's wrist as hard as I could. I felt my teeth piercing his skin, grinding against wrist bones and it sickened me but also, when I heard his shriek of pain, a fierce joy flooded through me.

How many kids have you hurt you stinking shit? How do you like a little measure of it back?

The gun dropped into the dust and he screamed with fury and fear and flung me back. I slammed against the sedan, my back connecting with the trunk lid. The breath went out of me with a whoosh and pain flared up through my back. Badass raised his bleeding hand to smash into my face, but Samuel was there, grabbing him, pulling him back, driving his fist into Badass's mouth as I sagged down on my knees. I gasped, trying to get the air back in my lungs, and then left the men to fight as I edged around to face the bungee cords. I blinked the sweat out of my eyes, grabbed the first one, pulled it off.

"No!" the driver screamed, and then the scream was cut short by the sound of fist on flesh.

I pulled the second and the third cords off, my hands shaking so badly I could barely control the elastic. I was determined, though, focused solely on those frayed green cords. I snapped the last off, closed my eyes briefly and sent a prayer heavenward, and then opened the trunk.

The small, pale hand lay on the filthy trunk carpet next to the strawberry blond hair. She was dressed in denim shorts, a white short-sleeved shirt, her feet in Princess Ariel shoes. Her eyes were closed, her face a sweet, still white, so still, too still, and an odd buzzing sound started in my ears and the sounds of the struggle faded as a wail rose inside me, a cry of such horror, grief and frantic denial as I saw that the eyes remained closed and the hand didn't move.

"Oh no," I moaned. "Oh please, no. NO!" I screamed, that single syllable reverberating down the hillside, echoing back denial and protest that anything should be so wrong, so unfair. I turned and saw the two men struggling by the side of the road, and the buzzing faded as the grief became a terrible rage.

"You killed her!" I screamed, and this time when I launched at him, I went for his throat, hitting and clawing.

Both men jerked in surprise, Samuel taking a half-step toward the van, and the sedan driver taking a half step toward the edge of the road. I drove my weight into him, hitting at his head and face. He threw up his arms and then he overbalanced and toppled backward, his arms pin-wheeling wildly, but nothing could stop his momentum, and he fell over the drop at the side of the road. In my blind rage, I nearly followed him, came so close to following him that for a moment as the strong hand grabbed my arm and pulled me back onto my feet, part of me still tumbled down that steep hill in the wake of the sedan's driver. In that instant I saw the man in black crash over a rock outcropping and through some dry bushes where he disappeared from sight, dirt and rocks falling in his wake.

"Are you all right?" Samuel gasped. "Are you?"

"No," I wailed and the bubble of rage burst and grief flooded in. I slowly collapsed down into the hot, soft dirt that powdered the road. "She's dead," I moaned. "We were too late. Poor sweet baby, poor…" and I could say no more as sobs welling up from the deepest part of me shook my entire body.

"Oh no," he said. "Please no. It can't be."

I heard his slow footsteps in the dirt, heard him slowly approach the open trunk. "Oh god, no," he groaned. I heard a stifled sob and then the sound of fist against metal.

I sat in the dust, the sun shining down on me.

Warm air, blue sky, gentle breeze.

I heard the ticking from the van's engine as it cooled.

I heard some birds down in the valley below us.

"Hey," Samuel said.

I shook my head.

"Hey!"

I couldn't move.

"Look, look!" He reached over and grabbed my shoulder and then forced my head up to face the trunk. "I think she's breathing!"

"Wha.."

"Breathing, breathing! Watch her chest. Watch!"

I struggled to my feet and looked into the trunk. I stared at that small white blouse, focused on the three little red and blue flower-shaped buttons, and then I saw them move, the slightest rise and fall.

"Did you see?" he shouted. "Did you see?"

I leaned over the trunk, staring fiercely, and the movement came again. "Yes! Yes! Oh my god, yes!"

We turned toward each other, grabbing each other's hands and began a jubilant dance of joy and abandon, tramping a circle, the dust puffing up, covering our shoes and legs, our shouts echoing off the hills.

"We did it! She's alive!" I cried.

"Damn straight we did! You were awesome! 'No fucking way,' and then you grabbed his arm!"

"What about you, walking right up to him, 'Got trouble, need help?' says Mr. Cool."

"When I saw that gun come out, and I thought that was it, my number, as they say, was up and you, you were like a terrier…"

"And you punching him, and he was going to whale on me and you stopped him…"

"Totally, righteously, awesome!" He grinned, grabbed me by the shoulders and kissed me.

Just for a second, it felt absolutely, perfectly right to have his lips on mine. Just for a second I thought…

Oh, that's what they mean

...then my hands came up and I pushed him away, frantic, grabbed his hands off my shoulders and flung them back at him. "I, no! I don't..." I stood, panting, staring up at him as the bewilderment grew in his face.

"But you were awesome," he said.

"No, I..." I felt my cheeks start to burn and I stared down at the dust on my shoes as the silence swelled and pressed against me.

"We should get her out of the trunk," I finally said.

"Yeah." I heard him move.

"I'll get her," I said.

"No, I will," he said.

"No," I said softly. "If she wakes up, she will not want to have a man handling her. Believe me," I whispered. I ever so gently pushed my hands under the girl's shoulders and knees. "It's all right now, baby," I cooed, though her eyelids never fluttered, her expression never changed to indicate that she was at all aware. "Everything's all right now. I'm going to take you to your mommy." I pulled her up with a grunt, and cradled her to my chest, shifting her so the blonde head rested against my shoulder. "Come on, sweetheart," I whispered. "No one's going to touch you. No one's ever going to hurt you again. I'll kill them first."

I heard a sharp intake of breath. "Whoa," he said. "I hope she can't hear you."

I eased the girl down into the booster seat and started buckling her in. "I hope she can." I clicked the belt and smoothed back her hair.

"Well, anyway, speaking of, well, uh, killing, do you think we should see if that guy, well..."

"I couldn't care less about that guy," I said. "I hope he's dead." I slid the door shut and turned to Samuel. "No, I'm wrong. I hope he's not dead. I hope every bone in his body is broken, compound fractures and he's lying down there in so much pain that he's praying to die, watching his blood pouring into the dirt, but I hope he lasts for a long time and when he finally dies he goes straight to hell and burns there."

"Jesus."

"What?" I said.

Samuel stood between the driver's door and the slope rising up from the road. His skin looked pale against his black hair, despite his tan. The red seeping from the abrasions on his forehead and chin contrasted starkly against his skin.

"What happened to you?" he asked.

I shook my head, looked down, and started dusting the dirt off my slacks. "Nothing, I got a couple of bruises…"

"No," he said, "what happened to you?"

I looked up and terror flooded through me at the kindness and compassion in his eyes. The words struggled to come forward, wanted to come forward and out…

NO, no, we're not going there! Never, never going there…

I looked him straight in the eye, not blinking. "I've known you, what, half an hour?"

"Yeah," he said. "A pretty intense half hour."

"Even so, does that give you the right to ask me, well, anything?"

He stared at me for a long moment then shrugged. "No skin off my ass," he said.

And I had the strangest impulse as I looked up into his face.

It's not that I don't want to tell you! It's not that I didn't feel something when you kissed me. It's because I did, because I'm so afraid…

I wanted to say it. Just for a second I wanted so badly to say it.

"What?" he said softly.

But then I thought of not his lips coming down on mine, but another's and I shuddered and stepped back.

"Nothing." I looked at the little girl through the dusty window. "Uh, since we don't know what he used to knock her out, I'm thinking we should get her to a hospital just as quickly as possible."

"Right. Okay," he said. He gave me one last enigmatic look, then moved around the front of the van to the passenger side and climbed in.

CHAPTER 5

I climbed behind the wheel, started the engine, started backing down the road, and stopped a few inches from the crumbling edge. I pulled forward, then put it in reverse and started to back again. This time I stopped with the left side of the van practically scraping rocks and the right side barely clinging to the verge.

"I don't think I can back down this road," I said.

He lifted an eyebrow. "Well, don't look at me."

"I thought all men thought they knew how to drive better than women."

"Not this one. Look at that road. My mama didn't raise no stupid children." He looked back through the rear window, then up ahead. "You think you can get past his car and find a place to turn around?"

I bit my lower lip and studied the sedan, half in the road. Sitting there motionless, the trunk lid flung open, it looked so much less ominous. But trying to get past it? I looked up and down the curve. Near the sedan, the road's left edge rose at not more than a 30 degree slope, and there were no major rock outcroppings. "I guess maybe I can drive up on that side and get by."

He looked back down the road and then to me. "Not much choice, is there?"

"No. You think you can move his car at all?"

He craned his neck, looked at the road, the sedan, the pine tree clinging to the sheer face. He shrugged. "Maybe. Can't hurt to try." He climbed out then leaned back in through the window. "Take it slow."

"Really?" I said. "I thought I'd just floor it, close my eyes and take my chances."

"No," he said, "I really think you might want to take it slow and easy. And you probably should keep your eyes open, too."

My lips twitched. "All right, smart ass. Just move the car."

"Yes ma'am," he said and saluted.

I glanced back at the little girl tucked up in the car seat behind me. She slept on, completely oblivious to anything going on.

Maybe she'll get out of this unscathed. Maybe she won't have to live with the horror.

The little girl murmured and shifted.

Alive, by god! We did it!

I felt the fierce joy coming back and couldn't help smiling. I watched Samuel walk up to the driver's side of the sedan and scan the road ahead, the slope next to the car, and then he walked back to the van and put one large, tanned hand on the door. "I think if I pull the sedan up a little, and you ease up that slope about halfway, then I can back it up and you can pull past."

"Okay."

He gave me an encouraging grin and then headed back to the sedan.

Man he's tall.

He slammed the trunk lid down, hooked one of the bungee cords to keep it down, and then sat down into the sedan. The old springs screeched under his weight.

He really is a big bear of a guy. Danny and Richie would love him.

I heard the old engine crank, trying to turn over. The tailpipe popped some black puffs and the car went silent. The engine cranked again, and again, and finally sputtered, coughed, and started. Blue-black smoke blasted out the back; steam started escaping from the seams around the trunk lid. Samuel eased the sedan forward and as close to the drop-off as possible. I followed, cranking the van's wheel, holding my breath as it tilted up the grade, tilting, feeling like it would go over, but if I held my breath and kept my whole body tensed, I could keep it from tipping too far. The side mirror hit the sedan and folded in with a crack, and I flinched and nearly twisted the wheel too far. I watched as the window on the sliding door passed a scant inch from the sedan's rusty roof.

Then the sedan began to move, backing away as I held my breath and eased the van forward. It dropped down flat into a blessedly clear, even place on the road. My breath came out in a whoosh, and I turned to give a congratulatory thumbs up. Samuel's hand came out the window, his thumb up, and behind his thumb was not an empty road, with dust and little else. Instead there was a head, then shoulders rising past the rear fender.

For a long, long second, I merely looked at that figure, unable to take in its significance, watching it slowly rise as Samuel turned off the sedan, opened the car door and started to straighten. The figure shifted and I finally moved, leaned out the window, screamed, "Look out!" as Samuel heard something and turned. The figure lurched toward him, swaying, blood dripping down his face, part of his scalp laying over one eye, something in his hand, the gun? Was it the gun? Had we really been stupid enough to leave it lying in the dust where he'd dropped it?

"Run!" I screamed. I reached up, hit the button for the sliding door and as it started to open, I dropped the van into reverse, stepped on the gas and rammed backward into the sedan. I heard a howl of rage and the report of the gun, their echoes overlapping as they bounced around the canyon. The van lurched as Samuel jumped through the sliding door behind me, landing with a grunt on the floor. I snapped the gearshift into drive and floored it up the road. The rear tires spun and then grabbed, spewing an enormous cloud of dust and rock behind. I punched at the door button three times before I connected with it and it slid shut with a satisfying click.

I was shaking again with fear, my stomach churning, the sweat prickling my skin again, but at the same time…

…a small version of me stood aside, observing all of this calmly.

Well, yes, of course, because nightmares don't end, do they? They go on and on, and just when you think you're safe, the door opens again.

"Are you okay?" I asked.

The van slammed across a rut and I heard a thud and a sharp cry. "Well I was," he said as he was flung into the seat back and then, as he tried to rise, his head bounced against the ceiling with a thump.

"I heard the gun go off," I said.

"Yeah, me too, but it went wild."

"Are you sure?"

"I think," he said as we bounced through a small ditch and sent a plume of muddy water into the brush, "I would know…" He gripped the backs of both seats, muscled his way into the front, and dropped into the passenger seat. He tugged at the seat belt, swearing under his breath until it clicked into place. "…if I'd been shot."

"Is she okay?"

He craned around and then smiled at me. It wasn't his 100-watt smile. No flashing white teeth, just a smile of sweetness and strength that warmed me, sent a tingling through me…

What is this? Stop!

Samuel said: "She's still out, but she's okay."

"Oh, good," I sighed and then started to ease up on the accelerator.

"What are you doing?" he asked.

"There's no need to speed on this awful road. He's not going to catch us… or is he?"

He flushed. "He might."

"You didn't take the keys?" I asked. "You left them in the car?"

"Well, I thought he was dead at the bottom of a canyon, now didn't I? And I figured when the sheriff got up there they'd need to move the car…"

"Okay."

"Who would have thought he'd come crawling back up out of there…"

"Okay, really. Okay. I probably would have done the same thing."

"Really?" he asked.

"Well, no, but then I'm a female and therefore just inherently smarter." I stepped down on the gas again, and we rocketed up the mountain.

He grinned.

I looked back to the road and concentrated on trying to miss the worst of the ruts.

"Inherently smarter, is that what you said? So, Ms. Inherently Smarter, why then are you out here in the middle of nowhere, driving a van over a road that would make a tank driver quail, being chased by a madman, having picked up a guy that was stupid enough to leave the keys in the bad guy's car?"

I sighed. "Well, in addition to being brilliant, I'm incredibly lucky."

"Yeah, remind me to ask you for the lottery numbers next Saturday. I could..."

A strange chirruping sound interrupted him, and then it sounded again, coming from the cup holder.

"My phone!" I yelled. "There's a signal. We must be high enough. For God's sake call 911!"

But he already had the phone in his hand and was dialing. "Wait, I can't hear anything."

"Can't hear...oh, the stupid ear piece, I must have dropped it and you need to use it or turn it off. Can you see it?"

"I'm looking..." he bent over, pawing through the CDs and socks, pushing under my legs and patting the floor...

Interesting how the touch of his arm on the back of my legs sends a shiver up my spine.

What is this?!

"I can't find it."

"Go through the menu, then and turn it off. Under tools, Bluetooth."

He punched at the phone. "Shit," he breathed. "Can't you keep the car a little steadier?"

"Oh, of course, absolutely," and I gunned the engine and plunged through a small ravine where some rainwater had washed away part of the road, and bounced up the other side.

"Thanks," he said. "Okay, ear plug turned off. 911."

He punched the numbers then hugged the phone to his ear. I could hear a tinny voice answer and he blinked and looked startled. "What?" he said into the phone. "I...I don't know. Wait." He turned to me. "Are you Jennifer Canfield?"

"Yes."

"Yes," he said into the phone.

. . .

"I don't know, on some dirt road somewhere off of Highway 28."

. . .

"You know where 28 is down to one lane at the construction site? About five miles after that, a right turn on a narrow road and then there's a metal bridge."

. . .

"I don't know, a metal bridge."

. . .

"The road forked after the bridge. We took the left fork."

. . .

"No, we have the girl with us. She's okay, except that animal gave her something. She's asleep."

. . .

"No, I'm sure. She's fine."

"Make them call her parents," I said. "Right now. They have to call them right now."

He nodded and told them, and then he listened, nodded and gave me a thumbs up.

"Well, we sort of pushed him off a cliff, but after we got the girl in the car, what's her name, by the way... Helen, sweet, after we got Helen in the car and we were leaving, he came back up onto the road and we took off."

. . .

"A small black pistol. I don't know if there was anything else."

. . .

"Stephen Baron."

I looked a question at him and he grinned and pointed at his chest.

"Okay, I'll try to stay on the line, but the reception has been a little problematic."

I rolled my eyes and snorted.

He kept the speaker at his ear but lifted the microphone end away from his mouth.

"Nice to meet you, Jennifer Canfield."

"The pleasure's all mine, Mr. Baron."

"So, 'Samuel Clemens St. James'?"

I grinned sheepishly. "I opened my mouth and that's what came out. Besides, you look like a Samuel."

"I do?" He looked down at himself. "I always thought I looked like a Stephen, but who am I to tell? After all, I'm just one of them poor, dumb, male-type creatures and you're a real smart lady-type person."

"True," I mused, "besides…" A sharp crack from the back of the van cut me off. "Oh hell, the back window just shattered! Damn it! Look, it's all crazed. We must have thrown up a rock or something."

"I don't think it was a rock," Stephen said. "Are you there?" he said into the phone. "He's shooting at us. He's coming up behind us and he's shooting at us!"

"Oh my god in heaven! This is never going to end," I cried.

"Go faster!"

"I'm going as fast as I can!" I yelled.

"I don't care," he shouted back. "Go faster!"

And somehow, I did. Driving a van over a road meant for a Jeep, slamming over ridges and ruts, bouncing so hard I could feel the springs bottoming out, but still keeping my foot down on that long, narrow pedal.

"Where are you guys?" Steve shouted into the phone. "Hey!" Pause. "Can you hear me?" Pause. "Shit!"

He dropped the phone down into the cup holder then looked at me. "They *are* coming."

"When, sometime tomorrow? Great, they can be here for the funeral!"

"We're not going to die."

"Tell that to him," I said, jerking my head toward the sedan behind. That ancient sedan should not have been behind us. By all rights, the engine should have blown, the radiator cracked, and maybe it had, but it wasn't enough to stop the sedan from hell. Black smoke boiled out from under the car, mixing with the dirt both cars were throwing up. Steam and more black smoke poured from around the hood, coating the windshield with splattered grease and thick brown dust.

"How can he even see?" I cried, but I saw how when I looked back. Through the dust I saw him leaning out of the window, pointing the gun, and then I saw the flash. "Did it hit us, did it hit us?" I shouted.

"I don't know," he yelled. "I can't hear anything but this van slamming up and down on this god-cursed road!"

"Is Helen all right?"

He gripped the arm rests tightly and looked back. "I think so. She's flopping all around, but the child seat is keeping her safe."

We topped the rise, and I was sure I was going to see the big valley ahead, with a line of cars with flashing blue and red lights coming up toward us. Instead we were heading down into another isolated valley. I could see the road we were on twisting down to the valley floor below, crossing a creek, and heading up into the trees on the other side.

A sudden whoosh and the crazed glass in the rear window bowed in and then blew out. Gummy cubes of tempered glass scattered across the dirt road behind us and sparkled in the sun like rhinestones. And it was then that I saw that the distance between the van and the sedan was increasing. Smoke and steam billowed furiously around the old car. "I think his car's finally quitting," I yelled.

Stephen looked back over his shoulder then flashed me a huge grin. "I think you're right!"

I kept my foot on the accelerator as we bumped down the twists and turns. Within a minute or two, all I could see of the sedan in the rear view mirror was a cloud of dirt and smoke coming up from behind one of the turns. "Holy crap, I think we made it." I grinned at Stephen.

"Wow. " He blew out a great blast of air and scrubbed his fingers through his hair. "Amazing."

No ring on the left finger.

Stop it! What do you care? You've been so careful. Don't let this guy get you off-balance.

No ring...

It's the drama, the excitement. This will pass.

(Maybe I don't want it to pass.)

I blinked. That was a new voice. And this new voice, this small, quiet voice sounded a great deal like... hope.

"No bars," Stephen said.

"What?" I looked at him, startled.

He held up the phone and I started to laugh. Maybe it was just the relief of feeling at last as if we were going to make it out of this alive, but once I started laughing, I couldn't stop.

"What?" he asked.

"No bars," I choked out.

He blinked at me, looked at the phone, and then started to grin. "You were thinking maybe I was ready to belly up to the bar and have a frosty one?"

I nodded and tried to get control of myself. "Sorry," I gasped. "It must be reaction."

"No, I think that's a great idea." He began to chuckle, and then to laugh. We were just reaching the bottom of the small valley and Stephen gestured ahead to an abandoned cattle chute flanked by broken, lichen-covered fence rails. A crow sat on top of the chute. "You go ahead and pull up at that next place and I'll get that fella to pull us a couple of tall ones."

We both brayed like jackasses and it felt good. No, it felt great. I checked the rear view mirror; no sign of the sedan from hell. I eased off the accelerator and the noise from the road settled to a more manageable level. The laughter eased to chuckles and finally just a few sighs.

"So," I said. "I want to thank you. I can't even imagine what I would have done if you hadn't been with me."

"You," Stephen said, "would have done just fine." He turned in his seat and studied me for several moments. I could feel my cheeks heating up again.

"What?"

"I don't think I've ever met a woman like you before," he said.

"Is that good or bad?"

"Oh, pretty damn good, I think. I've known a lot of women in my 38 years on planet Earth. Married one of them..."

Oh no!

"...though it didn't last but a few years."

Oh good.

"But I never met one who, well, how do I say this? I didn't know a woman could be as brave as I've just seen you be."

I blushed again. I shrugged and shook my head. "Lots of women..."

"Let me finish," he said. "I don't know that I've ever actually met anyone, man or woman, who would risk their life for a complete stranger. If you hadn't rushed him when you did, I'd probably be dead."

"Oh, I don't think I was so brave. I was just so damned mad." We eased down through a couple of deep ruts and then I gingerly started the van through the creek that flowed through the bottom of the valley. "I hope we don't get stuck," I laughed. "I'd hate to think about trying to get this van out of the mud. It's not really designed for this sort of travel. All these bumps and splashing through streams. Not what they had in mind when they designed the passenger van."

Stephen just sat and looked at me. "You have a problem with compliments?"

I shrugged and stared ahead. "Sometimes. Anyway, how much further do you think it is until we're out of these hills?"

"Not a clue," he said. He looked at me for another long moment and then turned forward again.

I eased the van through the last of the water and we entered a grove of pines mixed with oaks. It was instantly cooler and with the needles on the roadway, the dust blowing in through the broken back window dropped to almost nothing. For a few minutes, we could have been driving along any country road on the way to a picnic.

I looked at Stephen out of the corner of my eye. Big, strong, most definitely a man, sitting in my car, with me. What if...

The engine sputtered.

"What the..." I looked at the dash and for a moment I actually think my heart stopped. "Gas," I said. "We're almost out of gas." The engine sputtered again.

"Out of gas?"

"I was just going to work! I had a quarter tank! It was plenty."

"Of course it was. You had no way of knowing..."

"But he's still back there! He could still be coming!"

"Look, we've probably put at least a couple of miles between us and him." Stephen looked around then pointed ahead to where a stand of trees came up out of a cluster of huge boulders. "It looks like there's space between the rocks where the van might fit. Pull in there while you still can."

I turned and stared at him, wide-eyed. "Why, you want me to make sure I keep the road clear for him?"

"No! No. We try to hide the van so he doesn't know we're on foot."

"Oh, yeah, good!" The van's engine sputtered again and then caught. "Please, please, please, please," I whispered as I goosed the accelerator oh-so-gently. I eased the van forward, turning under the trees and starting into the opening before the engine finally died. "Time to push," I said, but Stephen was already climbing out.

I opened my door and planted my feet on the loamy soil.

"Ready?" he called.

"As I'll ever be," I said.

There are times in my life when I question the existence of a benevolent God, but this wasn't one of those times. The van rolled easily between the boulders and with just a slight turn of the wheel, it nestled down between two pines as if this place had been designed for my baby-blue behemoth.

Babe? Not quite.

Bluetooth. No.

I eased my door shut and walked to the back of the van. There was no sign of Stephen. "Hey!" I called as quietly as I could.

"Up here," floated down from the road.

"Can you see it?"

"If you're looking for it," said Stephen as he came down from the road. "Let's hope he's not looking for it."

"I don't hear anything," I whispered.

"Me either."

We stood for a full minute listening to the sounds of the forest. I could still hear the creek faintly in the distance, a couple of blue jay's arguing with each other, and the rustle of the wind in the branches above us. Though still relatively cool under the trees, the August sun was much higher now, and I could tell that the weather forecasters were probably going to be dead on correct with their prediction of 102 for a high. The warmth already penetrated the trees enough that the scent of earth and pine needles permeated the air.

"We'd hear it, wouldn't we?" I asked softly.

"I'd think so."

We both listened for another few seconds then turned to each other. I had to look up at him. He was at least a half-foot taller than my five-foot-seven. And he had the most remarkable gray eyes. They weren't truly gray; they had flecks of green and gold and his eyelashes were quite long and thick. A strange feeling washed through me, as if I'd seen those eyes before, which I hadn't, or I'd dreamed about them looking at me and if I kept looking I would know something or remember something or feel...

I blushed and turned away. "Let's get Helen out and get going," I said to the side of the van.

He cleared his throat. "Um, do you think you have anything to drink buried under that avalanche of toys and backpacks?"

In spite of everything, I laughed. "Probably. The boys are always taking a couple of swallows from water bottles then throwing them under the seats."

Helen's eyes were still closed, her chest still rising and falling in a most reassuring way. I shook her gently. "Helen?" Her head lolled back and forth, but there was no fluttering of eyes or change of expression. I looked over to where Stephen was digging several Hot Wheels and Matchbox cars, a McDonalds' Happy Meal toy still in the wrapper, and a few socks out from under the passenger seat. "She's still out. We'll have to carry her," I said.

"Eureka," Stephen said, and pulled out a nearly full water bottle.

I found two more under Helen's seat, along with a couple of sealed packages of fruit snacks. "And this is why a messy van is a great frigging thing. The next time someone makes a snide remark about my car..."

"Never again," said Stephen. He took the waters and fruit snacks, shoved them down in the Iron Man backpack, and slung it over his shoulder. He looked around and then down through the trees. "I don't know about you, but I'd like to get moving."

I nodded. My skin had begun to crawl with the sensation of being watched. I turned at the slightest sound and studied tree trunks or bushes, expecting a head to appear as it had behind the sedan up on the road.

"I know he's probably stuck up on the hill..."

Stephen gave me a look.

"Up on the hill," I said again. "He could have rolled the car all the way down to the stream..."

"...where he could be refilling his radiator."

I lifted Helen out, we both slid the side doors of the van closed, and met at the rear bumper.

"I'll take the first shift," Stephen said reaching for Helen.

"Are you su...?"

"Just give her to me." He took her out of my arms and laid her against his shoulder with one arm under her bottom. "Let's get the hell out of here."

"Give me the backpack, then." I took it, stuffed my purse in, pulled out the straps as far as they would go, slung it over my back, and followed Stephen up onto the road. We stood and listened. Green trees; sturdy brown trunks; pine-needle carpeted ground; shafts of sunlight filtering through the trees; tall, ruggedly attractive, black-haired man holding a tiny blonde-haired child in his arms.

He nodded and we turned and headed up the road, walking as quickly as possible through the warm morning.

CHAPTER 6

Unfortunately, Stephen's idea and my idea of walking quickly were quite different. He charged up the road, carrying a 40-pound child, and his breathing was perfectly level. I, on the other hand, was hauling my big, sorry rear end and a pack that couldn't weigh more than two or three pounds, and within ten minutes I was breathing like two-pack-a-day smoker. Granted, we're talking steep hills, but still. People say that when you're about to die, your life flashes before you. Well, I can tell you, when you're trudging uphill with no choice but to keep going, it's every time you bypassed the gym that flashes before you. Interspersed are evenings sitting on the couch scarfing Doritos.

It is not a pleasant experience.

"So," I whispered to Stephen's back, "worst-case scenario: he's down at the stream... getting his car working... and he comes blazing up this road... and mows us down."

"You're a barrel of laughs."

"Just wanted... to lighten... the mood," I said.

Stephen just kept walking.

"Sorry," I said.

"If he gets that car going we should be able to hear it," he said. "That'll give us a little warning at least."

"Agreed."

"Provided he doesn't spot your van's hiding place, he won't know we're walking. We should be able to duck off the road and let him drive right on by."

"Well, yes, agreed... but I don't think... this patch of woods... is going to last forever. Open hillsides up there. Not much cover."

"You have a better suggestion?"

"I don't know... Maybe... Hey... could you... stop for... a second?"

He stopped a few paces ahead and turned back. He looked down the road toward the creek, back uphill, and then at me. I stood, panting, arching my back then bending forward, trying to get my breathing even. "Well, first," I said, "I can't make it... with any speed up these hills."

"You're doing all right," he said.

"Liar."

"Well then, what? You want to just stand here until he comes along?"

"Hey," I said.

He shifted Helen. "There aren't a hell of a lot of options! I'm sorry you're so... I'm sorry you can't make it up the hill, but what the fu... what option do we have?"

I glanced at him, and then down.

"Sorry," he said.

I stared at his work boots. Brown leather. Splatters of black asphalt. Dark brown laces.

"Sorry," he said again.

"Okay."

"Really."

I shrugged and looked up. "Might be we're under a little stress."

He looked flushed and embarrassed. "Might be, but that's a poor excuse for being rude."

I smiled and shrugged again.

"So, are you ready?" Stephen said. "Giving him time to catch up with us seems the worst kind of idiocy."

"Well, besides the fact that my legs are about to give out, I'm thinking we might be making a mistake going this way."

"Why?" he asked.

"Well, as I see it, there are two possibilities: that sedan is dead, he's on foot, and he'll probably see the van; or he gets it going and comes up this hill and he probably sees the van anyway. We have to assume that he will soon know we're walking."

"Okay."

"And…"

"And," Stephen said quietly, as he shifted Helen up in his arms, "whether he has his car or not, or knows we're on foot or not, he'll expect us to keep going *toward* help, either on the road or alongside it somewhere."

"That's what I was thinking. We're pretty sure the deputies are coming, right?"

Stephen nodded.

"So basically, all we have to do is keep out of his way until they arrive. And the trees are thinning ahead."

"So, you're thinking circle back?"

I bit my lip and then nodded. "I think so. I mean, it's the last thing he'd think we'd do."

Stephen thought for a second. "I think that's a good idea." He smiled at me. "Which way, Scout?"

"South, methinks."

"South it is."

We headed off the trail into the trees, Stephen leading, blessedly following the contour of the hill rather than trying to scale it. Our entire conversation had been conducted in whispers; even so, as we headed through the grove, we stopped talking all together. I was sweating under the backpack and I saw that Stephen's shirt was starting to stick to his back. The top of Helen's blonde head showed just above his shoulder, gently rocking to the rhythm of his steps. While I had prayed earlier that she'd awaken, now I was praying just as vehemently that whatever that pig had given her would last just a bit longer. My boys were 3 and 7. I could just imagine if one of them woke up in a strange place in the arms of a stranger. In fact, I'd specifically taught them about stranger danger and the efficacy of a piercing scream. Richie (the seven-year-old) always added that he'd kick the guy in the balls. I told him that it wasn't nice to talk about balls or kicking someone, but if anyone ever grabbed him, he had my permission to kick like he was going for a field goal in soccer, except use his toe, not the top or side of his foot.

Most people don't truly believe that there are those out there vile enough to hurt children. Oh, they know it intellectually, but in the gut, there is something so repellent about the act, that even the idea of it has a hard time sticking. I was not "a lot of people." And, as I watched Helen's blonde head shifting on Stephen's shoulder, an idea began to form.

Maybe that's why I kept following. Maybe someone else wouldn't have.

Helen's head rolled slightly with each step, and in spite of the heat, in spite of the fear, the most incredible feeling moved through me. For the briefest moment, walking through that grove of pines, my feet crunching on the needles, the smell of resin filling the warm air, the web of all our lives seemed somehow visible and reasonable. Perhaps there was a purpose for everything that happened, good or bad.

Wouldn't that be amazing?

That tingling energy faded quickly, but a balance within me had shifted. I didn't know it then, but I would before too long.

For several minutes, Stephen headed straight through the trees, perpendicular to the road. As we moved out of the pines and into the brush and oaks, he planted his work boots carefully, avoiding sticks and crackling leaves as much as possible. I tried to stay in his footprints, but his stride was half-again the length of mine so it was quite literally a stretch. He stopped next to a lightning-blasted tree and leaned toward me. "Downhill now, I think," he whispered, then smiled reassuringly.

I nodded. His front teeth were slightly crooked. His breath was warm and smelled faintly of peppermint.

This is not the time to go through puberty! Get a grip!

But I think I like this.

Great, sure, but what is a big, gorgeous, intelligent, funny guy like this going to want with dumpy, screwed-up you?

And I heard his tense whisper again: 'I'm sorry you're so… I'm sorry you can't make it up the hill.'

I'm sorry you're so fat, was what he'd wanted to say. I'm sorry you're so fat.

From epiphany to falling down a black hole. I told the new, hopeful voice to shut up and I followed Stephen through the trees, trying not to cast even a shadow on the land.

"Jennifer!"

My head snapped up. Stephen was crouched next to a tree a few feet from the stream. I'd almost run into him. I dropped down into a squat.

"What's wrong?" Stephen whispered.

"Nothing," I whispered. I swallowed hard. "Nothing."

He cocked his head and looked at me for a second, then went on. "I'm starting to worry that we haven't heard any sheriff's cars or helicopters."

I looked up through the trees as if his words might summon a chopper out of the clear, blue sky. "How long has it been?"

He shook his head. "I don't know. I don't have a watch and I left my phone in my truck."

I swung the backpack off, fumbled through my purse, and then my hand froze as I got a vision of my cell phone, sitting in the cup holder in the console between the front seats. "I left my phone in the van," I whispered fiercely. "Stupid, stupid, stupid!"

Stephen shifted Helen carefully to his other arm, then shook out the arm that had been cradling her. "Stop it. You're not stupid. I didn't think of it either. Okay, okay. Regroup. We haven't heard his car."

"Right."

He smiled brightly. "Maybe the son of a bitch bled to death," Stephen whispered in the perfect tone of a child saying, *Maybe I got a pony for Christmas.*

I covered my mouth tightly to keep from snorting, and when I had control of myself, I gave Stephen a stern look. "Stop making me laugh. I'm not entirely sure I won't go into full-blown hysterics."

"Yes ma'am."

"He was bleeding. Part of his scalp was lying over his forehead. But scalp wounds look awful and it might not have been enough to stop him. We can't count on it."

"Noted. So, worst case scenario again. He's in fairly good shape, he's tracking us up the road, and the sheriff's deputies have the wrong location."

That sent a shiver over my skin in spite of the heat. "So, what do we do?"

Stephen absently lifted Helen's hair from her face and then patted her back lightly as he thought. "You know, we don't know how many of these roads there are through these hills, or how many steel bridges cross Landerson Creek in different spots. I made a wild ass guess that we turned 5 miles from the construction site. Maybe it was 8 or 10 and the deputies are scouring a whole other part of the mountain. We have to assume, at least for the present, that we're on our own. So I think we're going to have to get ourselves out of this. Walk out."

I nodded.

"So which way?" Stephen asked, almost to himself.

"Downstream," I said. He turned to me and raised a brow. I shrugged. "We can't go on the road. He's got to expect us to walk out either the way we came or the way we were going. When you're lost in the woods, you're supposed to stay put, but I don't think that's an option. So, we do the next best thing. His car is upstream. We go downstream."

Stephen regarded me for a long moment and then he nodded. He shifted Helen back to the other arm. He peered into her face and so did I. She still slept peacefully.

"Give her to me for a bit," I said.

"No, I've got her."

"For how long? Take a break. Did you forget? I've got two boys. I'm used to carrying them."

"Well, then, just for a few minutes."

I laughed very softly. "Don't worry. I'm sure in a few minutes I'll be more than glad to give her back." I reached out and he swung her around to me. I took her unconscious form and put her head on my shoulder, then hefted her up so my arms were under her thighs. For an instant, it was so much like picking up and holding a sleeping Danny that my eyes welled up.

"What?" Stephen whispered.

I smiled and shrugged. "I miss my kids."

"We're going to make it out of this just fine," he said. He hooked his hand through the strap of the back pack and straightened. "Lead on, McDuff."

I turned upstream and picked my way around the patches of rocks, reeds, poison oak, and saplings that lined the banks. It was fairly easy going at first, even with the extra effort of trying to move silently. The sound of the stream helped cover the sounds of our passage, and was really quite soothing, though it had an oddly rhythmic beat to it. The rhythm became a distinct thud-thud-thud and I turned to Stephen as he stopped to look up. Unmistakably, the beat of helicopter rotors was knocking on the walls of the little valley. We both scanned the sky, turning our heads like radar dishes trying to determine from which direction the sound came. It was impossible to tell and there was no flash of sunlight on metal against the blue sky.

Stephen leaned down close to my ear. "New plan. Find a place for you and Helen to hide while I haul ass up to the top of a ridge and signal them."

"Oh god," I whispered and my heart started to thump.

He looked up the stream then back at me. "I think it's the safest and fastest way out of this." The breath from his whisper caused a little flutter in the hair near my ear that tickled my skin. He leaned back and looked a question at me.

I took a deep breath and then nodded. He smiled and cupped my cheek with his hand. "I'll be back as quick as I can."

Just for a split second, I let myself feel the touch of his skin, then I straightened. "I'll…" I cleared my throat. "I'll keep going downstream until I find a place to hide," I said.

"Keep the backpack," he whispered. "You might need the water."

I rested my cheek against Helen's head and nodded. He helped me get the pack on, smiled, turned and started up the hill as I turned to head downstream. Three paces and I stopped to look back at him. When I did, he had stopped and was looking at me.

Be careful, he mouthed.

"You too," I whispered, though I knew he couldn't hear. He smiled, nodded and headed straight up the mountain as I turned back to the creek.

CHAPTER 7

An unconscious child is twice as heavy as a conscious child.

Within ten minutes my arms were throbbing and my legs quivering. I was searching everywhere for a place to conceal us, but it seemed the countryside was conspiring against us. No convenient caves. No large downfalls of concealing tree limbs. Just cottonwoods and pines and scrub brush too thin to conceal a rabbit let alone the two of us. So I kept walking. After Stephen had left, I'd continually swept my surroundings, including constant checks behind us. By the time we'd made it a half mile down the stream, I was simply plodding forward, concentrating only on putting one foot in front of the other. I shifted Helen from my left shoulder to my right and back again. For just a few seconds, the damp patch of blouse where her face had lain would feel cool before the heat and breeze dried the cloth.

I've always scoffed at books or movies where the hero or heroine gets too tired to keep moving when there is a mad killer on the loose. I no longer scoff. There is a point of exhaustion where the body simply cannot go on. For me, this point came at about a mile downstream between one footstep and the next. I stopped, blinking at the shaft of sunlight coming down through the trees, swaying a little, my legs and arms trembling, then I sank onto the loam underneath a small grove of mixed cottonwoods and pines. Thankfully, I was near enough to one of the larger cottonwoods that I could lean back against it and let Helen lay on my stomach and chest while my arms flopped at my sides. For a few minutes, I couldn't even scratch up enough interest to look back down the way we'd come to see if anyone followed. I didn't even try to get the backpack off. I simply closed my eyes, panted, and listened to the ringing in my ears gradually lessen to a distant chiming and then a low buzzing then...

I sat up, nearly knocking Helen off my lap. Something... what? An echo of a loud noise? I blinked.

I couldn't have fallen asleep... Yet, what happened? Something...

A shot rang out up the mountain and I realized it was another shot; the first had awakened me from my sleep or stupor or whatever it was. The terror washed away the last of my fuzziness. I clutched Helen to me, struggled to my feet, and peered up through the trees, scanning as much as I could see of the hillside.

How far away? Shooting at us? Shooting at Stephen?

I listened for shouts from a megaphone announcing the arrival of the cavalry, and looked for the glint of sunlight on metal. Nothing. Though my mind rejected the idea vehemently, I also listened for cries made by a wounded man.

And then, as my heart pounded and my head buzzed with fear, from down the stream I heard words that shall live in my heart forever: "Holy crap! Some asshole's up here shooting!"

It was a woman's voice rising above the gurgling of the water. I carefully looked around the cottonwood trunk. All I could see was brush, more trees, and sunlight flashing off the stream between the trees.

A male voice came faintly through the greenery, responding to the first voice which had been female. "Some idiot with a new toy, no doubt. Okay kids! We're going to have to cut the field trip short."

From further downstream I heard some childish voices protesting and groaning.

"Hey," I said.

"Come on kids, pack it up. It's a safety issue. Let's move it!" I could hear movement through the brush, heading away from me.

"Hey!" I said louder. I pushed off from the trunk and started walking toward the sound of salvation.

There were a few moments of silence. "Dave, did you hear something?"

"Yeah, a lot of kids bitching and moaning. Kids! Head for the vans!"

"No, something else."

"Hey!" I said again. "Hey! Help, please!"

"That! Yes! Is there someone there?"

"Yes!" I called. "I need help, please!" I heard leaves crackling, branches being swept aside, and then the sound of someone splashing through the creek. About sixty yards ahead, a young woman dressed in jeans and a bright yellow t-shirt came into view through some scrub willows.

I started to laugh as the tears began to spill from my eyes: an interesting sensation.

She started to hurry, and then to run toward me as my knees gave out and I sank back down on the ground. She came to a stop just in front of me, her face concerned and just slightly wary. Across the bright yellow t-shirt, Wilderness Adventures was printed. That just made me cry harder. Richie had gone to the WA day camp in town in June.

"Ma'am?"

"I… You need to…" I stopped, tried to clear my thoughts, and started again. "This little girl is named Helen. She was kidnapped from town. This man… a friend and I got her away from the guy who took her. The guy has a gun and he may have just been shooting at… my friend." I hugged Helen to me, stroked her hair, and then studied the young woman's face. She had a nose ring, several ear piercings, and kind eyes. I lifted Helen. "Take her, please. Get her and the other children out of here. He's crazy."

Her eyes widened. "Ariel shoes! Oh my God, the Amber alert!"

I nodded.

"What's wrong with her?"

"Drugged, I think."

The young woman took Helen, turned her around, studied her sleeping face, and then my (I'm sure) dirty, sweaty, tear-streaked, terrified face, and then lifted Helen up and laid her head on her shoulder. She turned toward the sound of children and adults downstream and opened her mouth. I frantically grabbed at her leg. "Quiet! Please, quiet! I don't know where he is. Just get the children and get out of here as quickly as you can."

"Okay, sure lady. Come on. You need help walking?"

"Yes, no, I mean, I'm not going…"

Idiot! Shut up! Go with her!

"…I need to help my friend."

"Pardon me lady, but are you nuts? Let's get out of here!"

"I… can't. Please get Helen out of here and call her parents, as soon as you can. Oh! Do you have a cell phone?"

"Yeah, but there's no signal back here. There never is. We come here all the time with the summer camp kids."

My faint wave of hope faded. "Okay. Go, please. Call the sheriff as soon as you can."

"Lady…"

I shook my head. "I can't just go off and leave him… my friend. Go."

"Yes ma'am." She gave me one last look and then started trotting back down the stream. A minute later I heard a couple of adult voices questioning, abruptly cut off. A few more minutes and I heard the distant sound of engines starting and more than one car leaving.

I thought of Helen in that car, rolling towards safety and I couldn't help but smile.

And then I thought of Danny and Richie.

What the hell am I doing?

CHAPTER 8

I made myself sit for a couple of minutes while I took stock: thirties, single mom, two boys, never took a course in wilderness survival or hand-to-hand combat, no weapon except an Iron Man backpack with three partially filled water bottles and a purse, exhausted, hungry, and terrified. I pawed through my purse and found a tattered tissue.

Who followed a kidnapper.

I wiped away my tears and blew my nose soundly.

Who faced down a man with a gun.

And the bravest yet...

Who let herself enjoy, no matter for how short a time, the touch of a man.

So you think you can do this? You're middle-aged, fat...

Shut up.

What?

Shut up.

And this time, I listened to the voice of hope. I was still exhausted, hungry, and terrified, but something inside had tipped the scales. Something inside was betting on winning instead of losing. I thought back to that brief epiphany. Perhaps something had shifted at that moment. And, even if I'd fallen into brief despair at Stephen's words about my... not being able to make it up the hill, the fall had been short.

I stood and brushed off the seat of my pants, adjusted the pack, and moved uphill away from the stream so I could hear better. The background thud of the helicopter rotors had been fading in and out. At the moment, the sound was gone. I heard birdsong, leaves rustling and little else. I didn't know where Stephen was. I didn't know if the gunshots had even involved him. I did know that if he were coming, he would look for me and Helen by the stream, so I intended to follow it back the way I'd come, perhaps this time with a little more stealth and certainly with a great deal less burden.

Walking toward danger is infinitely harder to do than running away. I'd always wondered about police officers, having to go into bad situations when the normal human urge was always to put as much distance as possible between yourself and any sort of danger. And here I was, heading toward a deranged man with a gun, who could be behind that gnarly-looking fig tree, or that squared-off boulder... maybe those blackberry brambles on the bank of the creek. Who could even now be drawing a bead on me, ready to shoot.

I stepped behind a pine and gave myself a firm shake. Literally. I shook out my arms and shoulders, kicked out each foot in turn and shook out the tension.

Panic is not going to help anything Jennifer Canfield. You're a big girl. Act like one.

I skirted around a tangle of underbrush and crept up the mountain a little higher. The trees began to thin out and I could see the land opening into fields of gold and brown wild grass scattered with boulders and punctuated with oaks. I kept to the trees, slowly zig-zagging between the creek and the open land, scanning for any sign of Stephen or Badass.

No. Not Badass. Dumbass. Shitass. Horse's ass.

I'd like to say that I rapidly conquered my fear and ended up completing my walk like a seasoned professional.

But that would be a lie.

I was so scared that I was dizzy. All the while I searched, a part of my mind gibbered and pleaded with me to turn and run until I could run no more. Another part of my mind insisted on flipping through a slide show: Stephen stretched out on the ground, blood soaking his shirt; Dumbass creeping up behind me, the flap of hair and scalp hanging over his forehead still oozing blood, his face drawn and white, his hand clutching that evil black gun.

"Stop it," I whispered, but my mind played by its own rules and right now it wanted to show me every horrible image it could. Unfortunately, I have a really good bad imagination.

So instead, I started thinking about the boys. As I crept around those trees and crawled through bushes I ran images through my mind: the day I met Richie, barely toddling, clinging to the social worker's hand, shaggy brown hair the color of a buckeye nut, a shy smile on his face. Walking into a different worker's office, seeing the baby carrier with Danny snuggled in it, an unbelievable amount of black hair sprouting on his three-week-old head, his tiny brown fists clutched in his blanket. The first words I'd said were, "He's beautiful," and he had grown more beautiful with each passing day. It had been clear from the start that I'd won the lottery when it came to my children. Objectively speaking, the smartest, most handsome, funny, caring souls on the planet.

My memories of that journey back up the creek have such a surreal cast to them: gut-twisting terror mingling with love and warmth.

I stopped in a copse of willows and took a small sip from one of the water bottles. The sound of the water spilling between the rocks below me was almost maddening and I wouldn't have minded guzzling down all the water I carried. Not knowing what was ahead, I forced myself to limit my intake. The sun shone almost straight down through the trees. Midday. Maybe four hours earlier, I had been tripping my way to work with only a quick stop to fill up on flour and sugar deep fried in fat, covered with more fat and sugar. Now, I sat, miles away, huddled behind some willow fronds, contemplating walking further into the path of a possible murderer while searching for a man I'd known for an hour or so.

A man who could be dead.

A powerful sense of loss flowed out of that thought, followed by a chill which shuddered through me and I swear reached into the marrow of my bones.

You only care because he's a nice guy. Because he helped you. Because you would be worried about anyone in this situation. "Ask not for whom the bell tolls..." That sort of thing.

Bovine feces, girlfriend.

"Not the time," I whispered. I half rose, peered through the leaves and scanned all around me carefully. No sign of movement. No sound that didn't sound normal. The faint thud-thud-thud of the helicopter was back, but it grew no louder.

Yeah, well how could it get louder? Stephen never made it to the ridge...

I shook my head sharply. I waited a good two minutes, then slowly and with infinite care made my way up the hill again. I was looking so carefully around and behind me, I almost ran into a dead tree. A dead, lightning-struck tree. The same tree we'd stopped at briefly, before turning toward the stream. I was sure of it.

We went straight down from the tree, and then Stephen went straight back up the hill, so he must have come this way.

Chunks of dead wood exploded next to my arm as the sound of a shot blasted the stillness. I screamed and fell flat.

"Bitch! I'll kill you bitch!" His voice. It screamed at me from all directions. It bounced off the hillside, the trees. I pressed into the loam, the leaves, shaking in terror.

Move Jen!

I can't!

Do you want to die? Do you want Richie and Danny to be motherless?

I started combat-crawling, scuttling really, digging my fingers and toes into the loam and using my knees and elbows to move up that hill faster than I would have thought possible.

BLAM! Another shot, its echoes and my scream blending. This time I knew the direction from which it came and I crawled left to get a pine tree between me and Dumbass. I sat back against the trunk, panting, blinking the sweat and dirt out of my eyes. I could hear him now, crunching through the leaves, making no effort at concealment. I stood up against the trunk, my fingers clinging to the rough bark, frantically trying to think. But there was no time to think; he was coming. I pushed off that tree and ran as though the devil were behind me.

As, of course, he was.

I heard a scream of rage behind me and another shot, but no searing pain, no exploding wood so I ran harder, dodging through the trees. I headed up-slope, but as I saw the trees starting to thin, I curved north back to the road we had originally travelled. My breath tore in and out, my throat raw, my chest heaving. My legs hurt so badly I was certain the muscles were going to cramp at any moment and I'd go sprawling in the dirt.

And then, I heard him shout again. Unbelievably, I was putting distance between us.

I must have hurt him when I pushed him off the road.

Excellent.

"Come back here you fat bitch!" His voice was growing weaker, and not just because of distance. I stopped behind a tree and leaned there for a few seconds, panting, trying not to collapse on the ground. I had to think. Blind panic had saved me this time, but next time it could get me killed. As my breathing slowed a bit and my heartbeat stopped pounding in my ears, I could hear him moving up the grade. He moved in spurts punctuated by cursing. Once it sounded like he fell, and that time he shrieked a curse most foul.

I peered cautiously around the trunk as I tried to get my breathing under control. My poor body had had quite the workout and had just about reached its limit. I needed to rest, I needed to find Stephen, and I had to stay out of Dumbass's way.

"You took her!" he screamed. "She's mine! Give her back!"

My stomach clenched at his words and for a moment I thought I would vomit.

"I killed him and I'll kill you!"

Oh no, oh please no.

"Tell me where she is!" he shouted.

I slumped back against the tree, my eyes closed, my mind feeling like a circuit breaker had tripped. Images of Stephen and Helen flashed, but they made no sense, I couldn't connect them to anything. I slid down the trunk, the backpack catching on the bark, and sat motionless.

"Ran away and left you, didn't he?" he called. His voice was weaker, but it still carried through the otherwise still morning.

My hands were palms upward in my lap. I studied the scratches and cuts on my skin. They were frosted with dirt and bits of leaf mould. I saw three broken nails. One was torn down pretty far, but I noticed that I didn't feel any pain.

I saw the scars on my left wrist and studied them as if they were a road map.

Uncle Bob won't come in this time. I been good. I prayed to Jesus and I listened to Mama and I done my chores. I never telled.

I traced the lines made by the razor.

He was gone but he came back. He came back. I can't... I can't... He'll never be gone. He'll always come back...

It doesn't hurt. I thought it would hurt...

And then the sound of the bathroom door opening and the look on Katie's face.

My head lowered slowly as my hands came up and covered my face. Seven when he'd left, fourteen when he'd come back. Mom had opened the door and screamed with the wonderfulness of the surprise. *Bob*, she'd said, *seven long years!* And she'd thrown her arms around him and he'd looked over her shoulder at me and smiled. I could still feel a terrible echo of the bottomless despair that smile evoked. I'd fallen in, and even after the hospital, the therapy, my sweet boys, it still felt as if I were falling, and had been since he first opened my bedroom door.

I sat against the tree in those hot woods, the sound of the maniac staggering through the brush and his occasional curses the only noise other than the wind and the stream. I thought of my boys, raising them, loving them. I thought of Stephen and me up on the road. I thought of hitting, kicking, biting, and then pushing that animal off the cliff. My head began to lift; my hands dropped away. I looked out on the dirt, the trees, the rocks. I looked up at the sunlight filtering through the leaves. My heart was pounding again, but for an entirely different reason.

At that second I knew beyond a doubt that I had stopped falling.

CHAPTER 9

I moved from tree to tree, letting the sound of his progress set my course. Knowing his location made it much easier to move. Having a goal made it easier, too.

Then he went silent. I froze, listening, but the cursing had stopped and so had the sounds of movement.

Passed out? Dead? Gone to ground again?

That last felt right.

I headed for where the road and the creek intersected. I would find his car. I would syphon the gas out and I would get it into the van and get out of here. I no longer had to search for Stephen, at least not alone. I would go and get help, and then I would come back and not stop looking until he was found.

I wiped my eyes, blew my nose, and plunged through the trees headed for the van. A gas can (empty) sat in the rear floor compartment in the van, and in all the myriad junk that littered the floor, I hoped to find a hose of some kind. If not, then I hoped the sedan from hell had something I could use. Otherwise, his gas tank was going to have a screwdriver stabbed through the bottom.

By the time I found the van, anticipation of attack crawled over my back. As unlikely as it might be that he'd caught up to me, or even knew what direction I'd taken, my head continually swiveled back and forth, checking behind me and to the sides. I almost wept when I saw blue between two trees, and then the familiar outline of the windshield. I stopped and listened intently, then slowly sidled up to the boulders flanking it. If he'd found the van, he might have done anything to it, even a booby trap, for all I knew.

He'd found it all right, but he hadn't booby trapped it. He'd trashed it. I couldn't believe I'd heard nothing.

Probably the noise of the stream.

The headlights were shattered. The driver's door stood open; the pig had urinated all over the seat and floor. A large branch lay next to the rear bumper, dark, bloody handprints on one end, the other end battered and cracked. He'd methodically smashed each window. What glass remained formed flimsy crystalline curtains that when touched shed glittering cubes onto the forest floor. He had completely violated my sweet, ugly, too-big van. My van. The van that had carried my children. I thought of Helen in the sedan's trunk. I thought of Stephen lying somewhere on the mountain.

"Motherf'ing bastard," I whispered. At that moment, if he'd walked into that space between the rocks and trees, I think I would have killed him with no hesitation and no regrets.

I found the gas can among the wreckage in the back, but no hose of any kind. My screwdriver lay under the front seat. As far as I could tell, he hadn't touched the engine or the tires, so my plan could still work.

As Stephen had theorized (just thinking his name hurt), Dumbass had rolled the hellish sedan down the hill. It sat midstream. Oil and dirt coated the grill, hood, and windshield. I waded into the creek. The cold water splashed over my hot, tired feet and calves. The driver's door stood ajar. I gingerly grabbed the handle and pulled. The door hinges kind of groaned and then let out a grinding squeal. I froze, listened, but heard no shout or sounds of movement.

Blood pooled in the driver's seat and had dripped off the steering wheel onto the filthy floor mat. Not nearly enough blood, in my opinion. A tool box lay open on the passenger seat with tools spread around it. A rapid scan of the back seat and floor did not reveal a hose of any kind. I pushed through the water to the trunk and there luck found me. Shoved into a back corner was a gas can and siphon hose.

A thief as well.

The can was empty, the hose intact. I have never siphoned gas, but having once taken care of a friend's home, the crawlspace of which flooded each time it rained, I'd become quite familiar with the principal of suction. In less than ten minutes, I had my can full.

Just as I threw the hose back in the trunk and pulled the trunk lid down, the strangest thing happened to me in a day full of strangeness: a shudder moved over me, raising goose bumps up and down my arms and a voice screamed in my mind: *Get away from the car! Get away!*

There was no room for doubt, no questioning. My brain, my whole body shouted, *RUN!*

I pulled the trunk lid down, hooked one of the bungees, grabbed tight hold of the gas can, and I ran up that stream just as fast as my legs would carry me. A thick clump of willows about thirty yards upstream was the nearest cover. I thrust myself into the middle. I sat as still as I could, breathing through my mouth, listening to the pounding in my ears from my frantic heart.

And I sat. A jay squawked from a nearby oak. Something small scuttled through the undergrowth behind me. And still I sat. Inside the willow bushes I could see nothing but green leaves and the sky above. I heard nothing but nature. Finally, after what seemed a small eternity, I crawled ever so slowly forward and parted some branches just enough to see the sedan. It sat where it had sat, the water flowing gently past. Nothing else moved.

Psychic warning my ass. You just freaked out, sweetheart.

I crawled backwards, grabbed the gas can and started moving slowly forward. A grinding shriek echoed up the stream and I froze.

The front door of the sedan! Thank you, God! Thank you for getting me out of there and not letting me crawl out at the wrong time. Thank you. Thank you.

I gently pushed the gas can into a niche and put one hand up to part the willow leaves.

Dumbass sat on the front seat, one leg hanging out, his foot still in the stream. It appeared as if he'd used his t-shirt as a makeshift bandage for his scalp, pulling it over his head, then tying the sleeves behind. The shirt may have been white, once. Now it was scarlet and brownish-red, scarlet where his scalp had torn and still bled. His arms were covered with abrasions and dirt. A large tear in his black jeans showed more bloodied skin on the leg hanging out of the car. He lay back against the seat and didn't move. His hand, with the gun loosely held, lay in his lap.

Stay or go?

The words cycled through my brain as I stared at that still black, white, and red figure.

Stay or go?

He sat up. He was doing something, I couldn't tell what, but after a minute or so, he started to climb out of the car. He hooked his left hand, still with the gun clutched in it, over the top of the door frame and pulled himself up. In his other hand was what looked like a wrench and a roll of electrical tape. He set them on top of the car then leaned slowly back in and pulled out a can of oil from the back floor.

Shit! He's going to fix it! Shit! The son of a bitch is going to get away!

Oh no. No f'ing way I will let that happen.

I backed through the brush, pulling the gas can with me. When I got out the other side, I crawled away from the creek, and when I was sure I was out of sight, I headed to the van. When I got there, I poured the gas in the tank, found some bags, sweatshirts, and a beach towel in the back and covered the glass and urine on the front seat. In the sweat-soaked, filthy backpack, I found the keys still sitting in the side pocket of my purse. I didn't once look around the clearing. I didn't once flinch at a noise. I was too angry to be frightened, and too determined.

Okay sweetheart, okay baby. You're going to start, right? I'm going to put this little key in and I'm going to turn it and you are going to start!

I twisted it and that lovely van started as if it had never been touched.

"Thank you, thank you," I whispered and put it in reverse. As it started to move, glass began to tinkle down from the windows. The engine noise bounced off the boulders.

I grinned with fierce pleasure when I heard a roar of protest from down in the valley. I backed out onto the road, put it in gear, and headed up the mountain. Only the empty seat beside me kept me from shouting with triumph.

CHAPTER 10

The windshield was still pretty much in place although star bursts of shattered glass made seeing problematic. Hot, dry air and dust came through the broken windows and the glass cubes kept falling. None of that mattered. I was moving and I was leaving that bastard behind.

The road passed out from under the trees and onto the hot, grass-covered hillside. It bore to the right, following the contour line of the mountain, paralleling the creek, below. Dust came out the back in a long brown plume. With each bump more glass fell, but the windshield didn't even quiver. (Long live the inventor of tempered glass.) With the wind blowing in, I wasn't too hot, but I was drying out quickly. I fumbled over on the passenger seat where I'd dropped the backpack and tried to pull a water bottle out. It kept getting caught on something. I shifted my eyes over for a second to try to see what, and just ahead and downhill a movement caught my eye.

"Oh shit!"

Impossible! He couldn't have made it up from the creek! He couldn't have! He...

I slammed on the brakes. The back tires tried to break into a skid, but the van shuddered to a halt still safely on the road. I leapt out of the door and ran like the furies were behind and heaven before me.

"Oh my God, oh my God." My eyes blurred and I wiped at them impatiently. When I reached the right spot on the road, I jumped down the hillside, almost falling a couple of times in my haste.

Below me, Stephen sat with his back against a boulder, the cuts and scrapes dark against his white face, but a huge grin on his face.

I skidded to a stop next to him. Pebbles and dirt tumbled down the hill. "You're alive," I panted.

"And so are you! Where's Helen? In the van?"

"I gave her to some camp counselors. They took her out. I heard shots…"

"So did I and I heard you scream."

"Oh, I screamed all right! Scared the you know what out of me but he missed me."

"Why didn't you leave with Helen?"

The rush of words dried up. I cleared my throat. "I… I couldn't."

"Why?" he asked.

I shifted my feet and made a show of looking up and down the road. "Because, that's why."

There was a long pause and then I looked at Stephen's bloodied face.

"He said he killed you," I said.

"Nope," he said and he grinned.

I dropped down on the dirt and dead grass and started bawling. Tears poured down my cheeks, my breath went in and out in hitching sobs, and I just looked at him and grinned and grinned and grinned.

"What are you crying about?"

"Nothing," I said and laughed through my tears.

He looked up at the road. "Your van's not looking too good."

"Tell me about it."

"How'd you get it going?"

"Siphoned gas from his car."

His eyes widened. "Are you shi… kidding me?"

"Nope."

"Wow."

I shrugged. "He wasn't there when I did it or anything."

"Do you have any idea where he is now?"

"Still down at the creek, trying to get his car to start I expect."

"He came when you were there?"

"Just after. Listen, I really don't think this is the time or place. Why don't we get out of here?"

"Good idea."

I stood up. Stephen didn't. "What is it?"

He grinned crookedly. "What isn't it might be easier."

"You can't walk?"

"Not too well. Left leg's busted. And the rest of me's pretty beat up."

I knelt down and looked more closely. I could see now that in spite of the smile, he was in a great deal of pain. His shirt and jeans were torn in several places and covered with dirt. "What happened?"

"I was high-tailing it up the hill and the SOB shot at me. I tried to jump behind a rock…" He shifted and looked down.

"And?"

"I tripped."

"Oh you poor thing!"

He looked up at me. "You're not going to laugh?"

I looked at him, aghast. "You're hurt! Why would I laugh?"

He shrugged. "My buddies would have ripped me a new one for doing something so stupid."

"Oh," I said, "and how many times have they rescued a little girl and then tried to keep from being shot to death?"

"Never Ms. Canfield," he said in a schoolboy's singsong.

"Oh shut up. How far did you fall?"

He leaned back and squinted his eyes at the sun overhead. "See that outcropping up there?"

I followed his gaze. About hundred yards up the mountain was a grouping of granite boulders. "You fell all this way from there?"

"Nope." He nodded his head down the slope and looked even more uncomfortable. "I fell all *that* way from there."

Just above the tree line was a clump of brush. I could just make out a spot that looked battered and torn. "Oh my God in heaven. You are dead. You have to be after that."

I looked back at him and he was studying his hands. "What, you're embarrassed?"

"Well, yeah."

I shook my head. "If we had more time, I'd make you tell me how a man who just risked his life to save a little girl could be embarrassed. But we don't. Dumbass might be coming."

On cue, we heard the sound of an engine grinding, trying to turn over, then silence.

I reached out to help Stephen rise, but he pushed my hands away. "Get the hell out of here!"

"*We* will," I said.

"No, you! Now! He thinks I'm dead. Great. I can hide. Get back in the van and go!"

"No."

"No?"

"No. Now give me your hand and try to stand. I'll help you up to the van."

He stared at my hand, then up at my face. I must have been quite the pretty picture: scrapes, dirt, tear stains, sweat, hair filthy and straggling down. It just didn't matter. I left my hand hanging in front of his face. A long, long moment later he reached up and grasped it. I leaned back and pulled and he rose up on his right leg, gritting his teeth and swearing under his breath. We heard the engine down at the creek try to start again. This time it almost caught.

Stephen put his hand on my right shoulder, I put my arm around his waist, and we started the hopping, jolting, sliding trip back up to the road. He tried to keep his left leg up, but it kept hitting a rock or dragging on the ground. I'd hear him hiss and then another string of obscenities.

"Sorry," he said, panting.

"Aw shit, that's all right," I said.

We weren't too far down, so it didn't take more than a few minutes to get to the road. We heard the engine crank twice. When we'd made it about halfway to the van, the engine below cranked, cranked, and caught with a loud backfire. We didn't even look at each other, just moved faster.

I grabbed the sweatshirt off the floor and tried to get as much of the glass off the seat as I could, then spread it out for Stephen to sit on. He took hold of the door frame and hefted himself up and I helped swing his leg in and set it as gently on the floor as I could.

I ran around, jumped in, and slammed the door. More glass tinkled down. I took hold of the key.

Please, please, please, please, please...

She started on the first try. I patted the steering wheel and stepped on the gas. "Good girl," I said. "Good girl."

Bluetooth? No, terrible!

Rocks and dirt spit out from under the tires and we headed up the canyon. It made me think of the Roadrunner in those cartoons, leaving a swirling cloud of dust. Dumbass would be the coyote. I just hoped an anvil would drop on his head. I started to giggle.

Stephen looked at me and I just shook my head. It was too hard to speak over the sound of the road and the wind. Besides, his face was pale and sweaty and I knew his leg must hurt abominably.

"There's water in the backpack," I said. He nodded and reached for it.

I checked the rear view mirror. "Get down as far as you can," I said. "He's coming."

The sedan still blew black smoke out the back, but the white steam no longer poured out from around the hood. I floored it, way past the speed where I felt in any way safe on that narrow road. But my blue beauty had the heart of a lion as well as eight cylinders and she roared up that mountain. We reached the crest and the van popped over the top of the hill, almost became airborne, and jounced down on the other side, and the most beautiful sight in the world appeared in the distance. We were over the last ridge of mountains that separated the little valley that held Highway 28 from the central valley of California. An open expanse of farmland dotted with a few small towns lay at the base of the foothills. Four-lane Highway 5, dotted with tiny trucks and cars was clearly visible stretching from south to north, beyond was the Sutter Buttes and behind them the magnificent Sierra Nevada range. But the most magnificent sight either one of us had ever seen lay just below, on the twisting road we were following, no more than 5 miles ahead: a half-dozen white cars with blue and red flashing lights on their roofs. Just ahead and above them was a helicopter, arrowing in our direction.

CHAPTER 11

"Now he'll have to drop back," Stephen said.

"You'd think."

Stephen craned around and I kept flicking my eyes at the rear view mirror. Instead of seeing a rapidly expanding distance between us, I saw Dumbass's arm come out the driver's window.

"Duck," Stephen shouted and I scrunched down, trying to bury my head between my shoulders while still steering the bucking van. The side mirror shattered and black plastic and glass exploded through the window. It hit my cheek, neck, and shoulder but missed my eyes.

Stephen grabbed my arm. "Are you all right?"

"Fine."

"Let me see!"

"Not now!"

He squeezed my arm and let it go.

"This has got to stop," I shouted. "He can't reload while he's driving, can he? He has to be running out of bullets. Is he running out of bullets?"

"How the hell should I know?"

"Well, you saw the gun."

"So did you!"

"But you know about guns, don't you?"

"Why the hell would you think I know anything about guns?"

"You're a guy!"

"And all guys know about guns?"

"Oh shit, I don't know…"

"No, you're right," he said. "I'm the fucking president of the fucking NRA and I got a gun rack in my Chevy and a shootin' iron in each pocket."

"Sorry," I shouted.

"I know," he said after a moment, still shouting above the roar of the cars and a clatter coming from under the van.

I tried to ignore the pain in my neck and face and tried not to feel like a bulls-eye was painted on the back of my seat.

The van suddenly jerked forward as a crunch of glass and metal came from the rear of the car. "He rammed us," I shouted. "The stinking lousy miserable son of a bitch rammed us!"

"He doesn't care anymore," Stephen shouted. "He's got to have seen the sheriff cars. He just doesn't care. He's pissed and he wants to take us out."

"Well I'm not going!"

"I'm with you!"

I wrenched the wheel to the left, dragging the skidding van through a tight turn by force of will, then wrenched it back to the right. Even above the clattering roar coming from the two cars, I clearly heard the thud-thud-thud of the helicopter. We dove through a grove of pines and there it was, hanging over the road waiting for us. I looked over my shoulder, sure now that Dumbass would drop back, but he didn't. He fired again and rammed us. I think the bullet went wild.

"Shit!" Stephen shouted. His leg had slammed into the bottom of the dash. He clutched at his knee and swore.

The helicopter swept around behind us and stayed over the sedan. "This is the James County Sheriff! Pull over! Now!"

Dumbass took a shot at the helicopter, thereby earning his name completely and, as it turned out, irrevocably. The copter swept up and off to the south while we continued on toward the string of cars.

"He's dropping back!" I shouted.

Stephen craned around to look. "Yeah! But, shit! Gun!"

BLAM! BLAM! BLAM! Followed by another smaller blam! from under the van. The rear suddenly slewed to the left, then right. I fought the wheel, trying to remember how to turn into a skid.

The sheriff's cars were no more than half a mile ahead. I just had to keep it together, keep it on the road, keep going, just keep going...

just keep swimming, just keep swimming...

I burst out in a hysterical laugh and I probably shortened Stephen's life by a few years.

"Dory! From *Finding Nemo*! I just named my van!" I shouted.

Oh yeah, that explanation made him feel better.

Clanking, grinding, clattering noises under the van. Jouncing over ruts, heads nearly hitting the ceiling. Glass cube curtains flapping and dissolving, shedding blue diamonds of tempered glass over us and the rest of the van. Trash and toys slamming around the floor.

Another tire blew, I don't know if from a shot, but the van very quickly became almost totally unmanageable. We were off the hill, farm land on either side of the dirt road, sheriff's cars roaring toward us. I saw Dumbass poke his arm out one last time with that black gun clutched in his fist and this time I hit the brakes. This time when he hit us, it was my idea. As soon as he connected, I stomped on the accelerator and headed off the road into a clear area and then fought to stop Dory before we flipped. It was close, but I got her to a complete stop. I threw open the door and looked back at the road. Dumbass hadn't followed us. As soon as we were out of the way, the sheriff's deputies had closed in and in a game of chicken, Dumbass lost. He tried to brake, went into a skid, the tires danced over the verge and the car rolled once, twice, three times before it slammed into the base of a giant oak and crumpled to half its size.

Two deputies carefully approached the tangled mass of metal at the base of the tree, hands on the butts of their guns, when there was a pop, a crackle, and flames puffed out from underneath. The flames grew, making a dull roaring sound which blended with the ticking of expanding metal.

A couple of the deputies ran back to their cars and grabbed fire extinguishers and headed cautiously down toward what was left of the brown and rust sedan, but by then, the fire was out.

"Didn't leave him much gas, did I?" I whispered.

CHAPTER 12

I walked around to Stephen's door. He lay back against the seat, his eyes closed, his mouth tight with pain.

I touched his arm. "You going to make it?"

His eyes opened and he slowly turned his head toward me. "Yeah, I think... oh my God your sweet face."

I put my hand up and felt slivers of glass and sticky blood. My hand started to shake. Then I started to shake.

"Come here," he said.

I moved over next to him and he put his arm around me. We stayed like that as the deputies moved up to the van.

"Ms. Canfield?"

I started to nod, but it hurt too much.

"Are you all right?"

I grimaced.

"You're Stephen Baron?" he asked.

"Yep."

"You hurt?"

"Yep," he said. "Leg's broken. Maybe a couple of ribs."

"Any bleeding?"

He looked over at the young deputy and lifted a blood-encrusted eyebrow.

The deputy laughed. "I mean any bleeding right now?"

"Nope."

"There's an ambulance on the way. You okay here for now?"

"Yep."

"How's Helen?" Stephen and I said together.

"She's at the hospital, doing fine. Her parents are with her."

I smiled at Stephen and he at me. I'd never been so tired and aching, and so completely filled with satisfaction.

I didn't look over at the sedan. "He's dead, right?"

"Yes ma'am."

"Okay," I whispered. My knees started to give out.

"Let's get you sitting down," the deputy said. He took my arm and started to lead me over to one of the patrol cars that they'd pulled into the dirt near Dory. I looked back at Stephen. "You going to be okay?"

He smiled, which only made my knees weaker. "Yes. Go sit down now."

"Yes sir," I said and went to sit and stay still for the first time in what felt like days.

Amy came directly to the hospital. "Oh my god in heaven," she whispered when she first saw me, and then she threw her arms around me and squeezed. And I squeezed back. I started shaking again and had to lay back on the gurney. The doctor stepped through the curtain surrounding the bed.

"Jennifer Canfield?"

"Yes."

She took my hand and looked at the wristband the admitting clerk had clipped on. "Your birthday?"

I told her.

"Are you allergic to any medications?"

I told her.

"Do you mind if I call you Jennifer?"

"No."

"Jennifer, you've been through a lot and you are shaking like a leaf. I'd like to give you a mild sedative while we clean your face and neck. Would that be okay?"

"More than okay," I said.

Whatever it was started working within a few minutes and just a little bit after that, physical and emotional exhaustion must have caught up with me. I fell asleep as they worked on cleaning and stitching the cuts on my numbed neck and cheek.

The boys were already at Disneyland, and I was finishing packing so I could catch the boat there. A stack of suitcases sat on the boat dock next to my bed. I pulled the top one up onto the comforter and popped it open. Pookieworm lay inside.

My heart took a sideways beat. "Oh Pookieworm!" I picked her up and pressed her to my cheek. Just as soft, silken, and warm, still smelling faintly of cinnamon. "Oh Pookieworm," I crooned and my eyes started to fill with tears. But then my hands were empty and Pookieworm was in the suitcase, now in the small pieces Uncle Bob had left her in. I grabbed the lid, slammed it down and shoved the suitcase off my bed and into the water.

The boat horn blew the first four notes of "It's a Small World." I waved at Mickey who was hanging out the porthole on the fifth floor. "Almost ready," I called.

"Jenny," he called in his high, piping voice. "You're going to miss the boat!"

"I'm almost ready!"

I took the next suitcase off the pile. It was quite small, much smaller than a makeup case. I found the tiny latch and opened it. Inside lay a utility razor blade. The cutting edge appeared to be rusted. I lifted it carefully from the red velvet lining and stared at it lying in my palm. "Small World" played again from the whistle, but I barely reacted to the sound. I ran one finger along the blade and felt a tremor go over my skin. I lifted it and tested the edge. I looked over my shoulder and saw the Matterhorn with the Disney flag on top. Standing on one of the snow-covered outcrops, Badass/Dumbass stood, his arms folded. At the base of the mountain, outside the gates, Stephen stood with Helen in his arms. Danny and Richie were with him.

"I thought you boys were in the park," I called.

"He won't let us in," they cried, and they were crying. They were terrified. I looked down at the razor and took it by both ends and pulled. It stretched, lengthening, and as I waved and twisted my hands, it formed into a mighty sword. On the river, the suitcase with Pookieworm was floating away. I dove in, the sword before me, and came up under the suitcase, cleaving it open with one swipe. Pookieworm grew out of the wreckage, whole, strong, and huge. I straddled her neck and she reared up out of the water and headed straight for the mountain. As I reached the boys, I swept them up behind me. Stephen leapt up behind Richie, still holding Helen. We crashed through the gates and headed for the mountain.

For a second, I couldn't find the hill, and then I noticed that it was only a few feet tall. The enormous size of the peak had been an illusion. Uncle Bob stood in his black clothes with his Badass tattoo trying to look big, but he was so small, so very small, and he was the worm and when Pookiedragon ran over him, he barely left a stain.

I opened my eyes and saw Amy sitting in the chair next to me.

"Not too bad," the doctor was saying to her. "Any scarring should be minor." She looked at me and smiled. "Back with us?"

I blinked and looked around the small cubicle. "I think so."

"As I was telling your friend, the scarring, if any, should be minor. We got all the glass out and everything looks clean. Just a dozen or so tiny stitches. How does it feel?"

I raised my hand and tentatively touched the bandage covering my left cheek and part of my neck. "Numb."

"That will wear off all too quickly, but I'll give you prescription for the pain."

"Thank you."

She stepped through the brown striped curtain to leave, but then paused and turned back. "That was a pretty brave thing you did today."

"Oh, well, thanks, but I think it wasn't so much brave as stupid." I laughed but the doctor didn't.

Neither did the nurse.

Amy glared at me until I blushed.

"Thank you," I said, and the doctor nodded and disappeared through the curtain.

CHAPTER 13

"My purse should be here somewhere," I said. I sat in a wheelchair while Amy poked around the room. She found my bag in the tray under the gurney.

"Anything else?"

"I don't think so."

"Well, then, let's blow this Popsicle stand."

She pushed me through the cubicle curtains and headed out into the hallway toward the big sliding doors leading out of the E.R. to the parking lot.

"Hey," I said. "Before we leave, I'd like to check on Stephen."

"Stephen? Oh, the guy. Sure. Let me find out where he is." She stepped over to the nurses' station and in no more than a minute we were rolling down the hall in the opposite direction.

Amy pushed the wheelchair like a pro. I hadn't even tried to argue against it when the staff had insisted I ride in one. I was more tired than I could ever remember, in spite of the short nap on the gurney.

That nap.

"What are you smiling about?" Amy asked.

"Nothing. A dream I had. I'll tell you later."

We rolled toward a set of double doors. The doors opened; a woman and a man holding a little girl stepped into view. They walked up the hall as we rolled down. They slowed as they approached us, eyeing me. The woman dropped her husband's hand and ran toward me, throwing her arms around my neck.

"Thank you thank you so much thank you."

"You're welcome," I said, clinging to her just as tightly. "I know. I have children. I know."

I felt her chest heave with sobs. She cried against my shoulder and there was no stopping my own tears. After a minute or two, she straightened, and we both laughed as we wiped at our faces.

She looked from her daughter to me. "Helen, sweetheart, this is Ms. Jennifer, can you say hi?"

Helen's green eyes looked at me suspiciously. "Hi," she said and buried her face against her father's neck.

"Hi, Helen. It's so very nice to meet you."

She gave me another quick peek, but that was all she was having of me.

Her dad stepped over, took my scratched up, band-aided hand and pressed his lips to the back of it.

"Thank you," he said.

I wiped my face, took a hitching breath and nodded.

"We'll see you soon," he said.

I nodded as the three of them walked past.

"Daddy," I heard Helen whisper, "that lady made Mommy cry."

"Sweet pea, do you remember when we talked about happy crying?"

Amy and I passed through the double doors, so I didn't hear her response.

Stephen lay on a gurney through the third door on the left. They'd taken his torn, stained clothes; he had a light blue hospital gown on. His face had been cleaned and bandaged. His arms had multiple gauze and tape patches. An air splint covered his left leg from above the knee to below his ankle.

"Hey!" he said and grinned.

"Hey yourself! How are you?"

"Fine. Well, you know…" He gestured at his leg. "They gave me something for the pain so I'm doing just great!"

"Oh, this is my boss slash best friend Amy. Amy, Stephen… wait a minute, wait a minute… Baron. Stephen Baron."

"Nice to meet you, Stephen Baron," Amy said and laughed.

"Nice to meet you, too, Amy.

"Jennifer, come over here and let me see you. How is your face?

Amy pushed me over near the bed. "Still very much there," I said. Stephen reached out and brushed his fingertips across the bandages.

"Ouch," he said.

"It's not too bad."

"Has your friend here told you what happened?" he asked Amy.

"Not everything," Amy said and gave me a look.

I cleared my throat. "I told you most of it," I said.

Amy looked at Stephen and smiled, and then back at me. "Maybe you left one or two things out."

I blushed.

"So," Amy said. "I need to go… get a drink. Dying of thirst. Be back in a minute, Jen and we'll get going." She locked the wheels on the wheelchair, gave me another look, and left.

Stephen gently touched the bandage on my cheek one more time and then let his hand fall back on the bed. "So," he said.

"So," I said.

"Did you see Helen?"

"Yes, I did," I said and smiled.

"Yeah," he said and grinned. "Yeah."

I heard the rumble of a gurney passing in the hall.

"Quite a day," he said.

"Yes. Thank you again for coming with me," I said. "I don't know what I would have done."

"You're welcome."

The loudspeaker overhead paged Dr. Dirks to Radiology.

"Jennifer?"

I looked up at him, met his eyes, and that glorious, frightening rush of feeling moved through me. "Yes?"

"You were incredible today."

"So were you."

"So brave."

"I've been braver."

He snorted. "When?"

I took a deep breath. "Now," and reached through the railing and took hold of his hand where it lay on the sheet.

He turned his hand and gripped mine. "You're trembling."

I nodded and tried not to cry.

And then he pulled his hand out from under mine. "Samantha! You're back! Jennifer, this is my… this is Samantha."

I looked up into the hazel eyes of a stunning brunette coming through the door. "Sammi," she said, looking at my hand still resting on the chrome rail. "Or if you have to, Sam. Only this one insists on calling me Samantha."

"So nice to meet you," I said.

She went around to the other side of the bed, leaned down, and kissed Stephen on the cheek, then sat in a chair there.

"So," Samantha said, "Stephen's only told me a little bit of what went on. I do want to thank you. Stephen told me he'd not be here right now except for you."

"Quite the contrary," I said. "I don't know what I would have done without his help." I looked at Stephen and then looked above his head, across the room, at the heart monitor beeping steadily.

"You would have done fine," Stephen said.

"Nah, not really."

Silence.

"Well," Samantha said, "in any case, thank you."

"Uh… you're welcome."

Amy came through the door.

"So," I said, "it's been good to meet you, Samantha. This is my friend Amy, Amy, Samantha. We have to get going. I just wanted to see if Stephen was okay."

I looked up at Amy and nodded at the door.

"Hey!" Stephen said. "When am I going to see you again?"

Samantha looked at him, at me, and then back at him again.

I shrugged. "I'm sure we'll see each other around." Then I made myself look him directly in the eyes. "Stephen, I can't tell you how much it meant to me to have you with me today. I don't know… I can't imagine…"

I nodded at Amy and managed to hold back the tears until she had unlocked the brakes and swung the chair toward the door.

"Jennifer, don't go. Stay and talk for a while... I mean... you know..."

"Stevie, I'm sure she's exhausted," Samantha said. "Let Ms. Canfield get home and rest. She's had quite a day."

"I know, but..." he said.

"Amy," I whispered and Amy pushed the chair through the door and down the hall.

CHAPTER 14

I pulled up the gravel drive in the rental car and parked under a large, fragrant cedar. Katie and Jon had left the porch lights on and as I switched off the ignition, the front door swung inward and a shaft of light cut through the darkness. The screen door burst open with a tortured squeal of hinges, slammed against the side of the house and one small and one medium-sized boy shape came bounding down the porch steps.

"Mommy!"

"Mom!"

I jumped out of the car and ran toward them and grabbed them both and swung them in a circle as Danny shrieked and Rich tried to look grownup and offended. I set them down and started kissing them all over their faces and Rich began to laugh and the three of us collapsed down on the pine-needles in a mass of arms, and hugs and kisses.

The screen door squealed open again and Katie and Jon stepped out on the porch.

"Oh my goodness I missed you," I said. "Never again. I'm never letting you out of my sight again. Even when you're 45 you still have to stay right with me."

"Mom," Rick groaned.

"Okay, Mommy," Danny giggled.

I gave them one last squeeze and then started disentangling and trying to rise.

"Mommy!" Danny cried. "Your owie is big!"

"Nah, it's not too bad. Just a lot of little owies with a big Band-Aid on it. That's all."

"Okay. I missed you Mommy do you wanna see the craft-and-art I did with the bine cones?"

"Absolutely! Come on Richie."

Rich stood, looking up at me with a scowl on his face. "Aunt Katie didn't say it was that big. She said you got a little owie."

I put my arms around his shoulders. "It is, Rich. Truly. The doctor just likes to put big bandages on because they pay her a lot more for big bandages than small ones and she's putting a swimming pool in her backyard and she wants to have a water slide."

He gave me a doubting look, then started giggling. "Sure, Mom."

"It's true!" I said. "They cost a thousand million dollars!"

He laughed.

"You all come on in the house," Katie called. "It's getting cold and the mosquitoes are coming out. I swear they're big enough this year to carry off a small cow."

"They won't carry me off, will they Mommy?"

"No sweetheart." I lifted Danny up and hugged him tightly. "Aunt Katie is kidding and besides, I would never ever let anyone or anything carry you off." I settled him on my hip and put my other arm around Rich's shoulders. "Neither one of you. Ever."

I rinsed the soup pot out and put it upside down in the drainer. I swept the last of the crumbs and vegetable bits into the compost and then I headed out to the front porch. Katie was just coming up the steps. "I will never understand why men and boys find the subject of farts so incredibly funny."

Down on the lawn, the boys and Jon were sitting in a huddle. The boys were giggling uncontrollably. I laughed. "Oh Lord! He's telling them the Herbie the Fart bear story, isn't he?"

"Yes." She laughed and then put an arm around my shoulders and squeezed. "It's been so much fun having them here."

"I'm so glad they *were* here."

She led me over to the swinging seat and we eased down into it. Up on the slopes of Mt. Shasta where Katie and Jon had built their home, it was just warm enough to be really pleasant in the shade. Blue sky stretched across the arch of the heavens. Mt. Shasta's snow-capped peak was the only white thing in the sky. The oak leaves in the tree that overshadowed the house rustled slightly in the breeze. Katie's flower garden, full of daisies, ranunculus, poppies, and a myriad of other dazzling flowers soothed and pleased.

"The press still hounding you?"

"Yes. But I don't think they know where I am and somehow, thank God, they didn't get my cell phone number."

"What made you do it, Jenny?"

I turned and looked at Katie. She smiled. "Are you ready to talk about it?"

I leaned over against her and put my head on her shoulder. "Yes," I said, and I told her everything starting with the donuts and ending with rolling down the hallway from Stephen's room with tears pouring down my face.

We rocked for a few minutes. "That dream," she said.

"Yeah." I smiled and sat up and looked at my sweet sister's face. "Yeah," I said.

"I'm so proud of you," she said.

I sniffed and wiped at my face. "Me too."

"So, what about this Stephen guy?"

I sighed. "Oh, you know. His 'friend' Samantha."

"You don't know how serious they are."

"They have to be serious. He let her call him Stevie. Yuck."

Katie laughed. "Or, maybe that was the final straw and he told her to take a hike."

"Well, if he did…" I grinned at Katie and blushed a little. "You know, I might…"

"Yes!" she said.

I jumped up from the swing and leaned out over the porch railing. "I think I see some boys who need to be tickled!" I called.

Danny and Richie squealed and jumped up from the grass as I charged down the steps.

"I'll hold them for you," Jon cried. He made to grab them and the boys screamed and ran.

"Don't worry, I'll get them!" I formed my hands into claws and started across the grass. "I'm gonna get you! I'm gonna get you!" They both laughed and darted across the brilliant green grass in opposite directions. I went after Richie, then darted after Danny.

My cell phone started ringing up on the porch. "Grab it, will you Katie? Tickle monster, tickle monster. Yeah, you better run!" They dodged behind the huge evergreen that shaded the lower part of the lawn. I could hear them giggling. I swooped around the tree.

"Jenny!" Katie called.

"What?" I yelled as I grabbed Danny, swung him around, planted him on his back in the grass, and started tickling him unmercifully.

"Phone!"

"Richie!" Danny called. "Save me!"

Richie jumped on my back.

"Ah," I called, "who is it?" I looked up at her trying to see past Richie's arms, which were wrapped around my face.

Katie was grinning. "Somebody named Stephen," she said.

Made in the USA
Charleston, SC
01 December 2012